P9-DDG-858

Shadow Lover

By
Hope C. Clarke

Author of Not With My Son and Best Seller

This book is a work of fiction. Names, characters, places and incidents are products of the author's imagination or are used fictictiously. Any resemblance to actual events or locales or persons, living or dead, is entirely coincidental.

Published by:

P.O. Box 1746, New York, NY, 10017
Phone: 718-498-2408   Fax: 718-498-2408
www.anewhopepublishing.com
email: NewHopePublish@aol.com

Copyright © 1999 by Hope C. Clarke

All rights are reserved, including the right to reproduce this book or portions thereof in any form whatsoever. For information, address Black Print Publishing Inc.

Library of Congress Catalog Card Number: 99-90760

ISBN: 1-929279-00-0

Cover Design: Keith Saunders
                m_asaund@bellsouth.net
Copy Edit: Sharron Nuckles
                smnediting@msn.com
Line Edit: Andre Saunders
                Andrsaunders@cs.com
Final Proof: Deidre Wall

Printed by: Quebecor World Lebonfon
                www.quebecorworld.com

Dedication

This book is dedicated to my dear friends Keesha Nance, Desiree James, and Dorothea Williamson. Thanks for being my motivation and inspiration. Friends like you are hard to find but easy to keep.

About the Author

Hope C. Clarke, is the eldest daughter of seven siblings who reside in Brooklyn, New York. She's a single mom who divides her time between being a full-time mom, employee of JP Morgan Chase and a devoted entrepreneur. When she isn't cultivating her nine-year-old son, or playing the role of administrative assistant, she utilizes her extra time writing and self-publishing fiction novels. She considers herself a Jane-of-many-trades as she has acquired education and training in many industries including accounting,. She is a licensed financial planner, multitasking in software operations, etc. Publishing, writing, promoting and marketing has now been added to her list as she introduces to the public her movie-style writing.

Hope Clarke has always been an advid reader of fiction novels. It was during her high school years at Norman Thomas, her English teacher noticed her skill in abstract writing. The annual Transcript published by Norman Thomas hosted a short story authored by her entitled 'The Day When The Big It Happened.' He also incorporated this story as part of the literary abstract writing for his English classes. This encouragement sparked the desire to continue writing. She has written more than fifty poems and short stories.Through her college years, Dean Koontz and Robin Cook are among her favorites.

Today, Hope Clarke encourages the development of talent whether it's writing, singing, speaking, dancing or whatever it may be. She is a firm believer that everyone has a talent and that it should never be wasted.

CHAPTER

1

The door swung open fiercely, almost coming off its hinges. Heavy thumping sounded on the floor as angry footsteps entered the house. An immense shadow cast its silhouette against the wall and floor. Backing away from the door, Angelica awaits her dark half. She had been in the kitchen preparing dinner, praying that she could make up for lost time and finish cooking prior to 6:00. With apprehension, she looked at the clock hanging adjacently to the door. Although the dew of perspiration stung her eyes, and she had difficulty seeing, her blurred vision noted that the clock read 5:59 with the second hand rapidly racing toward the twelve. Tick tock, tick tock, tick tock the red hand raced. It seemed to synchronize with the throb of her heart. In what seemed like five seconds was sixty and the clock now read 6:00...simultaneously, she turned off the burners...dinner was ready to be served. Just in time she murmured with a sigh of relief. Her life revolved around punctuality and schedule and late dinner was unacceptable. She hurriedly placed the dishes on the table, making certain that the utensils were in their proper place.

Dinner is ready, she said, in a voice so faint not even the sensitive ears of a trained canine could hear. Of course this was not the utterance of a secret jamboree but a plea for mercy. Today was the first time in a long time that dinner was not ready at least fifteen minutes before it was due. Towered by his formidable size, Angelica is struck to the floor!

"Noooo, please, somebody help me."

Her voice went unheard for there was no one around to hear her. Living in the country had its advantages and disadvantages. Privacy was one of the disadvantages for these impetuous beatings went unheard and unnoticed most of the time. On a rare occasion, a nosey neighbor over heard her perilous screams or caught a glimpse of her horrid beatings to no avail because people simply minded their own business.

Continuing to crouch in the corner while using her hands to shield her face, a series of blows descended upon her one after the other.

"Please stop," she cried through the cave created by her arms encircling her head.

Again and again the blows came, crashing down with immense pressure to the top and back of her head. On occasion when she came up for air, a blow would catch her already battered face. When he realized that she was protected from his fury, he snatched her up from her security position and flung her into the stove. The metal bit into her flesh and she let out a yelp. He raced toward her with one of his hands reaching out for her and the other clasped angrily in the air preparing to render a powerful blow. Angelica realizing the impact that this blow would carry, tried to flee but he caught her dress from behind and caused her to fall backward and strike the right upper portion of her head. A loud blunt sound followed and she lay lifeless on the floor. Angry eyes watched her, with fury and rage, while his anger diminished. His God given weapons had once again rained with hatred. Angelica lay unconscious on the floor with speckles of blood staining her blouse, the floor and the oven.

He now sat at the table, swallowing the bitter liquid

which had become the epitome of his destruction. His boss had just laid him off and there was no way he could feed his family. His job let him down and so did his wife. Every day he slaved for her, earning a living so that she wouldn't have to work. Most women would appreciate that, but not Angelica; she needed that sense of independence. Thinking over the events, he considered himself a reasonable man. He allowed her to have a job and mingle with her friends. His dad told him a long time ago that a woman's place was at home and the sooner you let her join the harlot gang, the sooner you'll lose her. A woman with friends can't be trusted. He had always been faithful to her and knew that she had dark secrets. For the past few weeks, she has been getting home late and not having dinner ready. Her routine has changed and her preoccupation with the soaps has definitely altered her personality. She was looking and he knew it.

Angelica remained on the floor. Her eyelids blackened and shut by the impact of his fists. Her body lay motionless on the floor. Ivan loathed what he had just done. Another day like many brought him home to terrorize his wife. His fists marked his strength and the emblem of his power. The voice he hadn't the guts to use in the workplace, he used to succumb the gentle, loving lamb that lie before him. No matter how hard he tried to justify to himself what he had just done, the outcome remained the same ... she was a good woman and his mind was over reacting. His jealousy was making him crazy and his obsession to control her had become inherent. He wondered why he hadn't just punched his boss. Instead, as always he came home and punished his wife for sticking by his side when he needed her the most. His fury subsided and the rage that had once again taken possession of him faded.

He noticed the foil-covered pan on the stove along with two smoking pots. Ivan wondered what she had prepared for dinner. He walked over to the stove to take a look. He lifted the cover to smell the pleasant aroma of freshly steamed vegetables; nicely browned ribs in a roasting pan were coated with homemade hickory smoked barbecue sauce... He could feel his stomach churning. Angelica knew her way around the kitchen and one thing she loved other than him was cooking. Dinner was never late and definitely not burned. Ivan hated burnt spots in his meals. When the smell of his home cooked meal filled his lungs, Ivan looked to see why Angelica hadn't come to fix his plate. Normally she would bounce back into action, but this time she didn't even stir. He returned his attention to where his wife remained. He knelt to the floor and slid his hands underneath her back and thighs then raised her from her from the floor. He carried her to the bedroom and placed her on the bed. Looking at her face, he became troubled at the blood clogging her nostrils. He hurried to the bathroom and wet a towel with cold water then returned to where Angelica was lying. Gingerly, he wiped at it until he had removed all traces of his ugly act. He didn't mean to hurt her. He had just become so enraged at his boss and needed to vent out. It just happened. As usual, the memory was vague. He really didn't remember doing it, he just knew that he did. It was as though someone or something had taken over his body and caused him to commit such an ugly act. Guilt ridden, he called her name...

Angelica. Angelica. Come on honey, I'm sorry; I didn't mean to hurt you. I promise I won't do it again."

Her lips remained shut. Not even a quiver was to be seen. Ivan became concerned. He raised her swollen eye lid and she stared through him with a blank, unknowing stare. He placed his hand under her nose to see if she was breathing. A very faint wisp of air escaped her nostrils. Fear stricken... "No," he cried and snatched her up from the bed then hurried her off to the hospital.

After being summoned to the emergency room, Dr. Painkin hurried to see the incoming patient.

"What happened here?" He questioned noticing the woman's right eye was swollen and blue. He also immediately recognized the broken nose bridge which was twisted irreparably on her face. There was a slow trickle of blood escaping from her nostril. The doctor pulled his penlight from his pocket shining it into her eyes. Immediately he noticed the imbalanced pupils. A secretion oozed from her right ear which didn't appear to be blood but when he carefully moped it up, a pink halo immediately formed around it.

"Shit, cerebrospinal fluid!"

His angry eyes looked up at her husband who stood there biting his nails wondering if he had struck her one time too many.

"Did you do this?" He questioned him. Before Ivan could answer, the doctor ordered the patient be rushed to radiology for X-rays. "I don't want any time wasted."

The two nurses at his side hurried the body down the corridor. The other summoned radiology to the operating room. A scan was performed revealing an acute subdural hematoma caused by a remote fracture which shattered under the surface of the cranium creating multiple brain lacerations and arterial tears.

"This is going to be a tough one. I want my team summoned right now." Dr. Frank said while examining the film. "She must have received a pretty hard blow for this type of injury. Take her to Trauma One and make certain she's prepped for surgery. I want her ready five minutes ago!"

Angelica was rushed to the first trauma room without delay. Her hair had been removed from the surgical area by the nurse prior to arriving to the surgical ward. The area had been cleansed and it was now the responsibility of the cardiologist and anesthesiologist to make certain the monitors are attached, and anesthesia administered.

In less than five minutes, Dr. Painkin entered the room with a trauma surgeon at his side. Because he specialized in neurosurgery, it was understood that this was his show and not trauma's. Also standing by for assistance was two surgical residents and a fourth year medical student. Nurse Green, the circulating nurse and best friend of Painkin looked on, alert for supply requests. There were five doctors surrounding Angelica's helpless body. A briefing was given to the other surgeons by Dr. Painkin and the incision spot was marked and opened. A thin incision was made to each layer cautiously until the swollen flesh was revealed.

"Look at the size of that thing," exclaimed Sherry Aredt. She had worked side by side with Dr. Painkin on three major brain operations since being on his staff over the past six months. As a resident, her surgical experience had heightened, but nothing could have prepared her for what she was seeing this very moment. Inside this woman's head was a hematoma the size of a golf ball, complicated by irreparable arterial tears. The increased swelling of the hematoma didn't make things easier as it continued to severely force the brain down into the brain stem. She was no expert but realized the desperate need for a miracle. If repair was at all possible, the patient would more than likely remain dysfunctional after the procedure. Sherry imagined that being a vegetable for the rest of your life was definitely worse than dying on an operating table.

"Damn, what am I going to do for this young lady? There is no help for her. She needs an angel of God to help her," exclaimed Dr. Painkin. He could feel anxiety and failure taunting him. He felt the acid building, racing to his throat. This beautiful woman was going to die and there was nothing he could do about it. There was a time he felt he could save the world and there was no problem he couldn't solve, and now a young woman would die on his table under his knife-his knife he thought again. The others looked at him for direction feeling the shared concern. No amount of study could have prepared them for this. Not one of them anticipated the disaster that lay before them. There would be six saviors going home with the same blood on their hands. A life lost who was beyond revival.

While the six stood around Angelica's head, deciding how to proceed, there was a seventh person in their midst. Although they could not see him, he was there, looking and observing what was transpiring before him. "You men have little faith-prayer without belief is useless." Looking from one to the other, he willed one of them to beseech his help. Without the summoning of the heart, his presence was void.

"What's this?" He questioned in disbelief. There was a despondent cry in the room. Someone loved this woman and was asking for help. Looking across the table, he spotted the unheard voice... Dr. Painkin had believed. He was asking that a higher power manifest its power and give this young woman another chance at life. He wanted to save one life from the hands of death and become her protector. Painkin had never seen her before but he felt an obligation and longing for her.

In hearing this, the power was granted. The unseen visitor's existence in this time would be short and his abilities limited, but he had sat long enough, watching this woman suffer at the hands of her husband. He didn't deserve her and certainly should not get away with it.

As the hand of the lead surgeon began the procedure, a miracle happened. His impotent hands made an attempt to stop the bleeding-it was remarkably easy. The clot was cleared and the pregnant tissue settled intact, in its proper place. Wondering eyes looked on in disbelief with renewed faith. Dr. Painkin could see the praise of his understudies. But what they didn't realize is that this is not a miracle by his hands but someone even higher who heard the covetous cries of his heart.

Her temporal readings were stable and signs of recovery which had been bleak were now promising. "Okay, everything looks good, let's close her up. Looks to me like another success story." Dr. Painkin said while his amazed eyes stared at the woman before him. Certainly, this must not have been her time. He knew that there was a greater power in the room with them watching over her because she was destined to die in surgery. When he saw that things were in place and his guidance was no longer required, he turned to leave the room and thought he saw a shadow walking ahead of him. He turned to look back at the others to see if they had noticed it. When he realized that they were diligently at work, he discarded the apparition as his imagination and figured he'd better keep it to himself.

Dr. Painkin cleaned up while staring at his reflection in the mirror, wondering if he was losing his mind. A tingle raced up his spine as his sixth sense told him that there was someone behind him. He spun around...

"Who's there?" He demanded looking wildly around the tiny scrub room...no one. Again he felt the dicey breath it was in his ear this time. A soft whisper spoke in his ear...

"Take care of her. Take care of this angel. She is now your responsibility."

Dr. Painkin searched again, he saw no one.

"Who are you? What do you mean take care of her? What about her husband?"

"Your request has been granted. Show yourself approved!"

Dr. Painkin waited for another response but received none. He beheld the shadow figure walking away from him. He left the room using a door which only he could see. He waited for something else or for a revelation but got none. The room was silent and no one else heard it.

Ivan paced the waiting room floor for hours waiting for the results. Signing the permission slip to allow them to operate on his wife was like signing her over to judgment. He looked at his watch and wondered if this nightmare would have a positive ending.

"How could I have allowed my drinking to destroy my life and the life of my wife," he cried?

The nurse only listened. He didn't deserve any kindness for what he had done. He should be punished; no one should get away with hurting someone like that. When he opened his mouth to say something else to her, she walked away and started pulling files from the cabinet. He would not find comfort from her. He would realize that what he had done was wrong.

After ten long hours, Ivan was notified by Dr. Painkin that the surgery was over and his wife was now in recovery.

"Your wife will be taken to intensive care where a close eye will be kept on her for about six to eight weeks."

Ivan listened intently as the doctor explained her remaining condition.

"Can I see her now?" Ivan petitioned in a whisper of a voice. He knew that everyone despised him but she was his wife and they had no right to keep him from her. The doctor sighed as he fell into thought. As much as he wanted to protect his patient from this vicious man, the law was against him. Ivan was apparently a clever man and was able to satisfy the questions of the police and evade an immediate arrest. Unless his wife confirmed their suspicions and pressed charges, there was nothing he could do about keeping him from his wife.

"All right you can see her, but only for a moment. She must remain at complete rest. She will not be able to respond to you, so don't expect one. Any sudden movements can cause her to go into shock and she may begin to hemorrhage. Do you understand?"

"Yes, I understand. I really didn't mean to hurt her, I was just so angry and..."

"Please, don't finish, I know exactly what happened next. It should never have happened." After that he walked over to the nurse's station and instructed her to show him to recovery.

"Come with me Mr. Carty." She escorted him down a very dimly lit corridor which seemed to have no end, he wondered if she was escorting him to hell.

"Are you sure this is the way?" he asked the nurse with apprehension. Ivan felt a chill he had never felt before. There was something cold lurking at his heels, breathing down his neck, taunting him, loathing him.

He tried to shake the thought but couldn't. He looked behind him, but saw nothing. It was there-something was there letting him know that he was hated and would not go unpunished-watching his every move. Even when he cheated on his wife, it was there threatening him. Of course nothing is said but he knew that something did not approve of him or his behavior.

The nurse looked back at him then continued in the direction she was going without answering him. Finally at the end of the hall, was a dimly lit room. Ivan slowly stepped into the room observing his surroundings as he entered. To the left of the room was a curtain pulled around what he presumed to be a bed. He heard a beeping noise coming from behind it. Cautiously he moved closer to the curtain wondering if his wife was really behind it. Then a thought flashed into his mind, he wondered if the hospital was plotting to kill him. Why would the curtains be pulled so tight? He wondered. He turned to look back at the nurse still standing at the door watching him.

"Look, do you want to see your wife or not? I don't have all day!" she said in an annoyed tone.

"Yes, I'm sorry, I'm just afraid of what I will see."

"What do you expect to see, you just bashed you wife's head in, do you think a miracle occurred during the past ten hours?"

Ivan felt a chill behind the nurse's statement. He finally stepped up to the head of the bed and pulled the curtain.

"Aaaaaah!" he shrieked. "Oh my God," he said backing away, almost running. The nurse watched him trembling like a sufferer of Parkinson's disease.

"What the hell is wrong with you Mr. Carty?" Her voice was strong admonishing him for almost knocking her down.

"What happened to her?" He stammered, demanding answers.

"That's none of your damned business."

"It is my business. That's not how she looked when I brought her here."

"How the hell would you know what she looked like when she got here? You don't even know her! Your wife's in the next bed!"

The woman was so heavily sedated that she didn't hear any of the ruckus going on.

"Oh, I'm sorry." Ivan said as he sheepishly re-entered the room bypassing the first bed avoiding any contact. He hurried over to the next bed where his wife lay with her head bandaged. The nurse fought hard to keep from laughing. He did exactly what she expected. She knew that he would look for his wife in the first bed. That patient scared her the first time she saw her. He's lucky he didn't defecate on himself! That patient has severe nerve damage which caused her face to puff up and twist in a horrifying way. Anyone would have responded that way if they didn't expect to see that.

Ivan had a lovely wife behind all those bruises but of course no one could see it because five long years had passed and not a week went by that she didn't suffer at his hands. And now, her beauty was concealed by white bandages. He held her hand, wishing that he could wipe away her pain. A tear found its way to his eye as he lowered his face to hers to give her a kiss.

"Mr. Carty, you're going to have to leave now." Dr. Painkin interrupted him with his sudden appearance and abrupt order. Loathing him, he remained in the doorway.

"All right, please take care of her. She's all I've got."

The doctor scrutinized him expressionlessly. "We'll do our best; of course you know it will take some time."

"How much time are you talking about?"

"As I said before, it will take at least a month. It all depends on her recovery and how she fights to get through this."

Ivan thanked the doctor and walked out the room. The nurse stepped aside to allow him to pass. The doctor checked her chart and told the nurse that it was time to administer her medication again.

Angelica, in her sleeping state heard a voice speaking to her...

"I have come to save you!"

"Who are you?"

"That isn't important right now; the only thing that matters is that you recover."

She squinted and strained her eyes to see the figure that stood in the shadows.

"If you are here to help me, why are you hiding from me?"

"Now is not the time for me to reveal myself. In time I will tell you who I am and why I am here, but for now, I want you to focus on getting better. Will you do that for me?"

"Yes. Are you some sort of angel or something?"

"No, not really, but if it makes you more comfortable, you can say that."

She started to ask him another question but he turned and walked away. In a whisper he responded...

"Your love-your savior is before you and he will protect you."

CHAPTER
2

Ivan heard the doorbell ringing. He pulled himself up from the lazy-boy recliner he was seated in and shuffled to the door.

"Who is it?" he called while looking through the glass panel on the door. A well-dressed woman stood there smiling broadly at him.

"Hi, Mr. Carty my name is Sandy, I'm a friend of Angelica and we work in the same office. Everyone at the office has expressed concern since we haven't seen her around in a few days and no one has contacted us to let us know if she was all right."

"Oh, I see, well Angelica has been away with her mother for a couple of weeks. Her mother had taken ill and she needed to visit her right away."

"That's strange, she never mentioned her mother being sick! Will she be all right?"

"Yeah, she should be back by the end of the month. If not, I'll give the office a call. I had been meaning to call in the first place, but I got tied up with emergencies of my own. I'll make certain to mention you stopped by."

"Thanks, I appreciate that."

He closed the door and watched through the window. She didn't seem at all convinced. He wondered if Angelica had been spreading rumors about him, provoking unwanted talk behind his back and whispering in his presence. On occasion when his anger got the best of him and led him to punish her, he always made up for it. Ultimately, he treated her well. He took her out to dinner and on exotic trips. They went dancing and he would always buy her flowers. What more did she want from him? He made up for the little misunderstandings and mood swings, but she knew the rules...what goes on behind marriage doors should remain private. Now what was so hard in that? He made a mental note to reiterate the rules when she returned from the hospital.

Ivan returned to the living room where he had been sitting and opened the paper to the help wanted ads. "A construction worker needed, must be a licensed welder-just the thing I've been looking for." Ivan picked up the phone and dialed the number under the position. "Hello may I speak with Bob?"

"Sure, may I say who's calling?"

"Yes, my name is Ivan Carty, I'm responding to the advertisement he posted in the paper."

"Which position?"

"The welding position."

"Hold on a moment. I think that position has already been filled."

Ivan waited until the receptionist returned to the phone.

"I'm sorry, the position has been filled." When she was about to disconnect, Bob called out to her... "Let Rich speak to the gentlemen on the phone, we may need another man."

Susan told Ivan that Rich would be with him momentarily.

"Hello Mr. Carty, what can I do for you?"

"I'm responding to your advertisement for a welder."

"What kind of qualifications do you have?"

"I graduated from F.I.T with an MBA in Electrical engineering. I also have a B.S. from Poly Technical College in machinery. I have background in plumbing, steam fitting, painting and drafting. I was foreman on my last job with a well known construction company Cushman & Wakefield."

"Seems to me you have just what we're looking for. That's a very impressive background. When can we meet?"

"How about in an hour?"

"Sounds good to me, do you have a resume with references available?"

"Sure do."

"Great, if things work out, I'll have you working tomorrow."

"See you in an hour." Ivan hurried to his closet finding his best suit which he meticulously ironed. He perfectly pressed a snow-white shirt which Angelica had pulled from the laundry only a day ago still perfumed with a choice fabric softener. Spinning the carousel, Ivan found an appropriate tie to compliment his suit. He took a quick shower then dressed just as quick before hurrying through traffic to his interview.

When he entered the office, Sharon told him to fill out the application she handed him. When it was complete, he placed it on the counter before her. She smiled at him while dialing Bob's extension.

"Hi Bob, Mr. Carty is here."

"Would you bring in his resume please?" She picked up the resume and walked into her boss's office. "Send him in please."

She returned to the reception area.

"Mr. Carty, Bob will see you now. Please follow me."

She escorted him to Bob's office. At the door, she

introduced him to Bob. Bob walked around the desk, shook his hand and greeted him in her most seductive voice...

"Mr. Carty it's a pleasure to meet you. I find your resume to be quite impressive not to mention your appearance."

Ivan was stunned as Bob approached him with her hand extended. Never in a million years would he have expected Bob to be a woman. She was beautiful. Her hair was wrapped loosely in a roll at the back of her head with long drop curls that fell onto her shoulders. She was cloaked in a pleasant aroma. Not like perfume, she smelled like a peach, ripe and ready to be eaten and by the looks of her, that's exactly what she wanted. He watched her as she returned to her desk.

"Have a seat Mr. Carty. Tell me a little about yourself."

He spoke briefly about his last job and other positions he held that he felt would be an asset to their company. She watched him, lingering on every word he spoke. He imagined her hands fumbling at his organ. She wanted him and he knew it. Even though her eyes didn't rest directly on his lips, he knew that she was watching them. Even though her hands which smoothed out her skirt in a slow tantalizing manner, he knew that the touch was meant for him. The aura was strong, the signal was there and Ivan knew he was the man for the job, both jobs.

"So, Mr. Carty, how does $100,000 sound to start? The job comes with perks." He smiled.

"What kind of perks?"

"The kinds that make a man go home smiling at the end of the day."

He waited a moment before answering as he

watched her teasing gestures. "Great, when do I start?"

"How does tomorrow sound?"

"I'll be here."

"Good, then I'll see you at 7:00 A.M. sharp, my place."

The boldness of the woman took him by surprise. It was one thing to suggest that she wanted to sleep with him but to outright say it was another. Now he wondered if this would be the beginning of habitual cheating. She stood up and walked around to where he was sitting with her mermaid shaped body and gave him the address where he was to show up at.

"All right, that will be all for today. I look forward to seeing you tomorrow. With your talents, I have a special job for you. I'm sure that you are the man I've been looking for."

Ivan stood up, shook her hand one last time and said he'd be there. Then she showed him out the office and back to the reception area. As Ivan reached the door, Bob yelled out to him...

"Come prepared to work, you'll get dirty." She then turned on her heels and reentered her office. When Bob was out of sight, the receptionist looked up at Ivan. Her eyes revealed the pending humor.

"I guess Bob liked you, you got the job."

"What job?" he questioned. Feeling her statement held more meaning than what she was letting on.

"Oh, you'll see when you get there?" She teased. Her eyes traced his structure and rested on his handsome face. Her statement caught him by surprise. Instead of asking her what she meant, he just thanked her and left the building.

Now having good news, Ivan decided that he would pay his wife a visit to see how she was coming along in the hospital. He parked his car in the parking area and made his way to the visitor's window.

"Hi, I'm Mr. Carty; I'm here to see my wife Angelica Carty."

"Just a moment please."

The woman typed the patient's name into the computer and when she had found Angelica Carty's room number, she handed Ivan a visitor's pass. He took the pass and went to the security guard that watched over the elevator bank. He showed the guard the pass and was given entry. When he reached the third floor, he saw a crowd of doctors surrounding a room. He looked at the floor map to see which direction would lead him to his wife's room. It was in the same direction as the crowd. She was in room 346. As the room numbers increased, the more he believed that they were surrounding her room. Finally, he reached her room and the doctors were in the room next to hers. Relieved, he entered her room. Angelica was lying in her bed resting. Dr Painkin, the doctor that operated on her was there talking with her. She seemed to be all right, although the bandages were still there. Her face had almost returned to normal. The bruises were practically invisible. He would never take his frustrations out on her again. She did not deserve that; he would strive to be a better husband to her. "Hello sweetheart, how are you feeling?"

Simultaneously Angelica and Dr. Painkin looked up at him as though to say, how do you think? When she didn't respond, he moved closer to the bed and asked the doctor if everything was all right.

"She's improving, but it's only been a week."

This was the first time Ivan came and found her eyes open. She had been sedated on all of his other visits and the doctor discouraged any disturbance in her rest. The doctor remained in his seat next to her bed.

"May I speak to my wife alone?"

Dr. Painkin looked to his patient for approval. She nodded in approval. He squeezed her hand then turned and walked out of the room. Ivan moved closer to his wife and took the seat once occupied by the doctor.

"Angelica, I know that you are upset with me and I don't fault you. I'm terribly sorry for what I have done. I should have never taken my anger out on you."

No response came from her. "I had lost my job after a heated argument with my boss and I lost it. Instead of coming straight home, I stopped at the bar and got a couple of drinks. I didn't know that I would come home and hurt you"

She still gave him no answer. Angelica had nothing to say to him. He wasn't sorry about what he had done, he's just realizing that he's alone and there is no one for him to punish when things weren't going his way.

"Angelica, please forgive me. I'm working hard to get better. Things will be a lot better. I have a new job that is paying a lot more than I have ever made before. We won't have to struggle anymore."

Angelica wasn't concerned about the money; she would have been content with living in a cardboard box with yesterday's news covering the door than to live with her violent husband in a mansion. "Listen, I promise I will never hit you again. Can you give me just one more chance? If I hit you again, I will leave you alone myself...I promise."

She still just stared at him with a puddle of tears blurring her view of him.

"I know that the doctor must have filled your mind with things. They're trying to convince you to have me put away. But honey I know that you know how much I love you and that I only want the best for you."

With all Ivan's pleading, Angelica never changed her expression. She was far from understanding him. He almost killed her this time. She imagined what would happen the next time he became angry. Dr. Painkin told her that she should let him help her. Let him save her from this monster before it was too late. But she knew all to well that Ivan would never let her go. He would never allow her to break the vows she made to him. The thought caused her to shiver. The sound of footsteps caught her attention and she noticed Dr. Painkin passing by.

Ivan didn't like Angelica's silence. This doctor seemed to have too much influence on her. Then he thought about it, wondering why the doctor was taking so much interest in her and her well being. Was he trying to take his wife from him? Did he want his Angelica? He moved his chair closer to her bed and she flinched.

"I'm not going to hurt you. Are you that scared of me? Listen, if you want me to go, I will. Just speak to me, don't leave me here wondering where things are going. I love you. Nothing else will matter without you." He stood up and towered over her. She sank deep into her pillow while pressing the buzzer to the nurse's station. A fleet of doctors and nurses came rushing into her room.

"Are you all right Mrs. Carty?" Nurse Green asked as she wedged herself between Ivan and the frightened patient's bed.

"Would you have Mr. Carty to leave my room?"

The nurse looked at him and told him that he would have to leave.

"Angelica, you called the nurses on me? Why?"

She remained in her frightened position. "Mr. Carty, please leave. Don't you see that you are scaring your wife?"

"I'm not scaring her; the doctor is trying to steal my wife! I want him to stay away from her."

"The doctor is doing no such thing. He has only tried to help her get past the emotional scar you left her with."

"I will have her moved from this hospital if you do not stop interfering in our marriage."

"Not without the request of our patient. Mr. Carty perhaps you aren't aware of the crime involved here. If your wife wanted to, she could press charges against you. Battery not being the greatest offense but attempted murder and we will see to it that you will serve a life sentence."

"Nurse, you are out of line and I suggest you stand down." He turned to Angelica who was at the present gripping her sheet.

"Ivan, please don't make things difficult. All the nurse is trying to say is that I need time to heal".

"No!" He insisted emphatically. "I know what's going on here. I can see how the doctor watches my wife. If he continues this, I will..." letting his words trail off and biting his bottom lip. Nurse Green stepped two paces backwards out of his reach before speaking.

"Mr. Carty, your wife asked you to leave. Don't make me call security." Ivan looked at his wife one last time to see if she wanted to change her mind. When she remained silent, he gave a scornful glare at the doctor then stormed out of the room. He carried his fury home and again, found the bottle. He couldn't believe that his wife would turn on him like that. He would win her back. She was still upset about the last time.

CHAPTER

3

Ivan got up at 5:00 A.M. to prepare for his first day at work. He pulled out his work clothes and boots. He found the card she gave him with the address on it. At 6:30, he pulled up in front of his boss' house. He couldn't see any work to be done on the outside. He parked the car then rung her door bell. After a few moments, she answered the door.

"Boy, you're here early, come on in. The others will be here soon."

At 6:45, four more guys were escorted in. She began her introduction of the men to Ivan.

"Paul, Robert, David and Jimmy this is Ivan. He will be in charge on this project."

They shook his hand and welcomed him aboard. Then she escorted them to the rear of the house. Right away, Ivan could see what needed to be done. She wanted to extend her home toward the back and add an outdoor pool probably like the one he saw being done a few homes away. It seems as though everyone in this neighborhood tries to keep up with each other. Bob could see that her intuition about Ivan was correct; he picked up what needed to be done. She knew the others probably didn't have a clue.

"So, is all of this space to be a part of your pool or are you going to put something else out here?"

"Most of it, I'd say about fifty feet of it. The balance will be for lounging. Ivan, have you done this kind of work before?"

"Certainly have, not on a residence but in a hotel resort."

"This will be my little resort."

"What are the estimates for time and cost?"

"What will your pool be made of?"

"Marble."

"That's different; don't you think your guests might bust their asses on that? Are you sure that's what you want?"

"Oh yeah, my uncle had his done the same way and he hasn't experienced any problems with it."

"All right, then let me suggest the ground be a slightly textured concrete to prevent slipping."

"That's fine, but I want the marble, I prefer the classy look."

"Then I'd say this will cost you about one hundred seventy grand for the marble itself. Then the equipment and machinery rental will probably run about another five or ten grand. Finally, there's the cost of cement, cleaners. I'm sure with this size pool, you don't want to have to clean it yourself, and so you will have to have a cleaning system installed. I'd say the total job will run you about one fifty on the high side plus labor."

"Fine, come with me, I will have a special checkbook made up for you with a three hundred thousand balance. I want a running log of each expense. Order whatever you need. I want the job completed as quickly as possible. How long do you think it will take?"

"If the guys I'm working with are good, it shouldn't take any longer than three to four weeks."

"Sounds good to me, any problems with the workers let me know and I will have them replaced. If you require more man power, I will hire more men. Of course, I will let you screen them."

Ivan called the guys together so that he could explain the job and what needed to be done. He designated responsibilities and told them that the fewer men he needed to hire, the more money they would make.

"Let's try to keep as much of it as we can. Anyone have questions?" He waited for a response, when he received none; he presumed he was understood. "Good. Since you fellows don't have any questions let's do some shopping."

He took the men with him to Outback Furnishings where they purchased twenty cases of peach pearled marble to match her patio decor. Ivan knew that a woman of her caliber would be pleased with it. She seemed to have good taste and liked things to be unique. He would make it exceptionally special. He gave the address to the store for delivery. Then he met the guys outside with the truck. They took care of the cement and other materials needed for the job. Finally, he took his credentials to an equipment rental store and rented the machinery required for the portion of work to be done the first week. After that, he and the guys stopped off for lunch.

"So Ivan, how long have you known Bob?" Jimmy asked him.

"We just met yesterday when I interviewed for this job."

"Yesterday, she must have really liked you. She didn't start you on any outside jobs?" David was surprised. All the others started off working in the field on projects like office buildings, restorations on clientele homes. Never in three years of knowing her, has she taken someone off the street to work directly in her home not to mention give them access to company money. Normally all materials were ordered by her or Richard.

"No, like I said, yesterday was my interview. She told me that I would start today at her house."

"She wants you man." David teased. This was the only thing that made sense to him.

"This is strictly a business situation. I'm not interested in anything else, besides isn't she married?" Ivan inquired. This was all too amusing to him the way these guys were carrying on about their boss.

"Nah. She likes a well-stocked man, especially the married ones. It's all about control." David continued.

"No woman is going to control me!"

"That's what you think man. Look at your salary. Are you getting paid an exorbitant amount for the work being done? That's her way of buying you. No one wants to give up a well-paying job even if he has to sell himself to do it. She must have seen right through you. You need this job and that means you need her. She will call you right in the middle of love making with your wife and demand your presence. She has perfect timing, somewhere in her mind there's this device that says, he's getting laid, I better call." Robert joined in.

"You guys are spineless. I don't believe you don't know how to handle a woman."

"Just wait until the day is over, you'll see. She'll ask you to stay awhile and then she'll begin her game of passion. And as far as wives are concerned, trust me they can smell it if you've been fucking around, and you know what that means...No more honey for the bee. You can kiss that happy home goodbye." Robert concluded, slapping five with David and Jimmy. Paul only shook his head. He knew that Ivan wasn't listening to their non-sense anyway. He stayed out of the Bob debates and horrors. He's had his share of her and he thanked his God that she hasn't looked his way since.

"Anytime you sleep with a woman it should be a pleasurable event. However, I can assure you; she will not come between me and my wife. No one will."

"Okay man, you'll see what I mean." David said with a deep throated laugh.

"No, she'll see what I mean."

They all looked at him as if to say, "Seeing is believing." They would see if he was as cocky tomorrow as he is today.

Back at the house, Bob was preparing Ivan's initiation to the job and its perks. When it was time to leave, all the guys gathered their things and made their way to the door when Bob called Ivan back. Jimmy whispered to Ivan...

"Now the fun begins."

"Don't worry fellows, I'll handle her. She'll be meek as a lamb the next time you see her."

They laughed and told him so long. Ivan turned to see what Bob wanted to discuss. When he entered the room, Bob stepped close to him. Her breath was hot against his lips. It smelled fresh, winter-fresh. Ivan stood still to see where she was going with this.

"I promised you some perks. Are you interested?" she mused.

"That depends on what you're offering." He responded, never removing his stare.

Bob fondled his groin receiving no response.

"What are you impotent or something?"

"No, you didn't say please."

Ivan immediately lifted her up onto the bar. He pulled her skirt up over her hips then tore her soft silk panties away. They cascaded to the floor like a feather in the wind. Then with a box cutter, he sliced the tiny rhinestone surrounded by pearl buttons from her jacket, revealing her Victoria's Secret. Of course it was no longer a secret for he had just discovered her mounds of passion.

"Please," she said with reluctance.

"That's more like it."

He pulled her hand down to his groin again so that she could see that he was fully functional.

"If you want it, then you'll take it my way!" he told her with a wide cocky grin.

"I want it." She lusted.

He opened his pants and freed his staff. He grabbed her with both his hands at the sides of her face and fiercely, yet passionately kissed her with his tongue. His tongue moved aggressively and sweet inside her mouth. Meanwhile his hands stroked his throbbing penis and he spilled his hot semen on her furry mound. Then he spread it around both on the inside and outside of her vaginal lips. Ivan shoved his member into her with one back-breaking thrust. Her scream came as no surprise; he knew that she would enjoy him. She wanted him to be rough. He would satisfy her years of discontent. Make her forget all the spineless men who were too afraid to give her the pain, the pleasure she so desperately needed. Her desire to control was only a front. What she really wanted was someone to take charge. She released so sweet.

"That's how you want it, isn't it baby?" He questioned her. He worked his body in a circular motion, hitting her deeper with each thrust. "Ever been fucked in your ass?"

"No."

"Good, then I'll be your first." He turned her over making her legs hang over the bar. He pulled her cheeks apart with one hand then spilled his liquid all over her buttocks. He placed his penis to the opening of her rectum then with one strong thrust, entered her.

A yelp escaped her lips and she gritted her teeth to fight the pain. With smooth motions, he stroked her walls.

"Damn you're tight." He pulled back until he almost came out then pushed forward at a curve and she screamed...

"Baby don't stop! Please don't stop!"

He had found the hidden spot. She was going crazy. The pain she initially felt had turned into a pleasure she had never known. She could feel her ass and pussy coming together. His own release shot out of him like a canon.

"Damn your ass is good. Shit for me baby, shit."

He started spanking her until all had come from him. He gave one last thrust then withdrew himself. He took the towel off the bar's counter and wiped his dick then turned her over pulling her off the bar. He lifted her up and thrust into her vagina again.

"You like that don't you? Say it. Tell me how it feels. No one's fucked you like this have they?"

She couldn't catch her breath. He was hitting all her spots. G-spots she didn't know she had, he was hitting them, and hitting them hard. Every orgasm was like a chain reaction. They came one right after the other until he finally stopped. Like a brute, he dropped her to the floor.

"Where's your bathroom?"

She looked up at him puzzled.

"Upstairs to the right."

He went upstairs to take a shower. Just as he got the water right and stepped in, the curtains opened. Bob was standing there with the stink of their escapade. She lifted her leg to step in.

"Uh uh, you wait till I come out. This isn't a love affair. You wanted a fuck, you got it. It's over now.

Don't you know I'm married?"

A surprised look replaced the relieved one. He must not have realized that she was the one who would be writing his checks. "Do you know who you're talking to?"

"Sure, I know who I'm talking to, the question is do you know who you're talking to? Did you think you would control me? Have me jumping at your every beck and call?"

She just looked at him stunned. How dare he talk to her like that? She would fire him.

"Ivan Carty, do you think you're not expendable?"

"No, I'm sure my job is expendable. Don't disturb me while I'm taking my shower!"

He closed the curtain and she sat on the toilet seat watching him through the curtains, waiting for him to come out. She wondered if this guy might be crazy. The thought of him being crazy made her fear for the first time. She grabbed a towel and went to her guests' bathroom to take her shower. Now resenting him and repulsed by his fluids, she couldn't allow it to stay on her a minute longer. When she finished taking her shower, she returned to her bedroom where she found Ivan lounging on her bed as though he was at home. This angered her. Who in the devil did this guy think he was? She wondered.

"Get dressed and get the hell out of my house," she demanded with vehement.

"Get out, that's what you say to a man you just seduced? So you mean to tell me you love 'em and leave 'em? Is that it?" he said twisting the situation. His humor in the matter was not amusing to Bob at all. She was not going to play this game with him either.

"No, I don't love them and leave them, you cocky son of a bitch."

"Calling names I see. It seems to me that you're upset. Didn't I please you? Fucked you like you've never been fucked before. So why are you so upset?"

"You have no respect, that's why." Her words were like a small dog barking; So much anger with very little power.

"Respect, you want me to have respect for you after what you've just done? Lady, please. You don't want respect, you want control and you can't have it; At least not with me. Maybe you have David, Jimmy, Paul and Robert wrapped around your finger but not me baby. I already have a wife and she doesn't have control over me."

Bob was fuming..."You're fired," she screamed racing toward the bed where Ivan was casually laying. As she reached the side of the bed where Ivan was, he snatched her by the arm causing her to tumble onto the bed with him. He quickly positioned himself on top of her and forced her legs open with his knees.

"You're right, open your legs and let me have some more of that."

Ivan aggressively took her again. His passion was insatiable. He placed his hands around her neck and began to squeeze while forcing himself into her. He hammered and stroked her, grinding into her warm cave until he could feel her sweet release. Although she was gasping and fighting for air, it didn't hinder her orgasm. Her body collapsed against the sheets. He extracted his penis.

"Next time thanks would be in order."

Bob didn't respond. Her once widened eyes had shut. She didn't move when Ivan climbed off of her. Ivan figured she was just angry. He went back into the bathroom and quickly washed himself. He returned to the room and gathered his clothes. He looked back at

Bob.

"Hey. You still aren't speaking to me? You know you're really a cold woman. I fuck you, make you cum and still you are ungrateful. Look at you laying there all stiff." He teased her. "What's your story? Why are you so damn bitter?"

When he finished dressing, he returned to the bed. He leaned down to kiss her, but she didn't budge.

"You okay? Say something. Should I come to work tomorrow or not?"

Nothing. Her body lay stiff. Ivan shook her. Her body moved but only because he was shaking her.

"You're no fun."

Ivan turned to walk away, but his instinct told him that something was wrong. He looked back at her and placed his fingers on her neck. He frantically searched for a throb. He didn't find one. He grabbed her wrist, nothing happening there either. He used the back of his hand to feel for breath.

"Oh shit. The bitch wasn't as strong as I thought she was."

He started pacing the floor. "What am I going to do now? This is the last thing I need. With Angelica in the hospital and the hospital threatening to press attempted murder charges...I got to fix this."

Ivan knew that he needed to cover his tracks. He would be the prime suspect of this murder if he didn't think. Then it came to him, the perfect getaway for the perfect crime. After dressing, he went into her bathroom and filled her douche bottle with soapy water. Placed her into the bath tub, washed her from head to toe, and then cleansed both her rectum and vagina with betadine until it was squeaky clean. When he was finished, he placed her on her bed under the covers to keep her body warm. He turned her heating blanket to a low setting making certain her body remained warm. He cleaned the bar and anything that would leave traces of him sleeping with her including shaving her vagina to make sure there were no hair particles left behind. He drove down Colver Lane about thirty minutes away from Bob's house to a poverty-stricken area. He noticed a slew of bums down an alleyway. He continued past them and there was one who stood out from the rest. He was alone and seemed to just be misplaced.

"Hey man," he said to a man laying on a cardboard box. "How would you like to make $200 bucks?" Ivan had a wild crazy look on his face.

"What do you want...to fuck me in the ass? Well I don't do that kind of thing. They say that hurts you know?"

Ivan frowned with disgust. "No, I don't want to fuck your stinking ass. I have a job for you?"

"Well, what is it?"

"What do you care? You aren't working anyway."

"I still have my pride."

"Forget it." Ivan started walking away when the man hurried over to him.

"What is it you want me to do?"

"Fuck a dead body." Ivan's statement was all too forward but he figured what did he have to lose? He would go to jail if he didn't. He didn't have time to waste playing charades.

"That's too creepy for me man. Find someone else to do that shit. What are you some kind of fettish porn producer? Get someone else to do that shit."

The man's response let Ivan know that he had considered it. He pressed a little further.

"Too creepy for five hundred dollars?"

"Hell yeah it's too creepy for five hundred dollars.

What if she had AIDS or some other heinous shit? I'm a bum, but I don't want to die!"

"Nah. This is a clean bitch. I'll give you one thousand dollars in cash, small bills. That's enough to at least get you cleaned up and get your life started again."

"Man, you can't even rent..."

Ivan cut him off. "Look, take it or leave it. I haven't got all day. It's more than you got now. "

"I guess, she won't mind, she's dead anyway. Am I going to be arrested for this?"

"With this lady's caliber, they would never suspect to look for any one of your likes to be in her house. The woman lives in a mansion. There will be no way of tracing this back to you. One thing, I want you to get cleaned up first. I don't want the police or forensics to find any filth in her house or on her. They would definitely think someone she didn't know came in there. And if that scent you've developed gets into her house, they would definitely start checking this neck of the woods out. Catch my drift?"

"You get off on making people feel small don't you, a real control freak?"

The man looked at Ivan with contempt but because he was offering him a second chance, he decided he would bite his tongue and go along with it. It was in his favor anyway. Ivan drove to a local store, purchased the man a couple of outfits, some soap, cologne, shampoo and a pair of clippers. He then drove to a local hotel and told him to get cleaned up. He needed to hurry before the body hardened. When he cleaned up, Ivan cut his hair and took a good look at him.

"Now this is how you should remain. If you are smart, you will use the money wisely and maintain your appearance. Don't let yourself get down like this again. He took him to the car; blind folded him so that he wouldn't know the directions, recognize the house nor the woman.

"Why is all this necessary?"

"Because if I don't I will have to hunt you down and kill you. The less you know the better off you'll be. If you don't recognize anything, I don't have to worry about you being a witness or suspect."

When Ivan pulled up into Bob's driveway, he led the man into the house and to the bedroom where Bob was laying. Ivan placed his hand on her and was pleased to find her body was still warm and soft.

"She's still good for you. Do what you've gotta do."

The man stood there with his eyes covered. Ivan led him to the body.

"I can't do this man. My dick won't even get hard!"

"Beat it. I don't care what you have to do, just make sure you cum in her."

He swallowed then positioned himself between her legs. He stroked himself and thought hard about how she must look. He could feel her firm legs; her mound was clear of hair and her flesh soft. He put his fingers to his nose. She smelled like peaches. Oh yeah, he thought, this is a clean bitch. Suddenly, he felt it coming. He shoved himself inside her and started hammering away. Ivan watched as the man found an ecstasy he'd probably forgot existed.

"Take her how you want her man, she won't protest." Ivan goaded the man on. "You ever got a woman in the ass. You ought to try it, there's nothing like it."

Excited, the man turned the body over and pressed his way in.

"Damn. She just shitted."

"Ugh." Ivan said frowning, "there's your cue, you'd better hurry up, get out of there because rigor mortis is setting in and you might get locked up in there!"

"Damn," he exclaimed. "What the hell had she been eating?"

"I don't know but I'd wash that shit off right now. Here's a wet towel."

Ivan handed him a towel and the man wiped himself clean. Bob's body made a sudden jerk as her body began to stiffen.

"Time to go partner." Ivan led the man out of the house. He took him along with the clothing he purchased for him to a rooming house. "Listen, you forget this ever happened and get your life started again. I know I promised you a thousand dollars, but I'm going to give you five. Take care of yourself and never be too proud to do a job. Of course, when you get your humanity back, you won't have to be subject to this kind of thing again. Just think of me as your dark savior."

He handed the man the back pack with his toiletries.

"The money is in there. Don't be a fool."

He told him holding his hand out for the man to shake. He shook his hand then walked out. The man looked back at the stranger. Ivan had in his own way become a friend to him. There was no humiliation left in his being for where his days had once been dark and bleak a new light had shone through. He walked up to the clerk and requested a room pulling money from his pocket for the first time in years. Tomorrow, he would search for accounting work for which he had worked in for years.

Ivan walked away with three hundred ninety five thousand dollars in a checking account just for him.

Since it was a personal job, the company could not reclaim the money. As far as he was concerned, there was no real record of what the job required. He would return to her house tomorrow as though nothing had happened. Of course, the guys would find her first.

CHAPTER

4

"Angelica, how are you feeling today?"

"I'm all right Dr. Painkin. How about yourself?"

"I'm fine now that I see you."

Painkin didn't know exactly how that slipped out but now that it had, he wasn't about to take it back. He would let fate lead the way.

"What did you mean by that?" Angelica asked not wanting to make any assumptions.

"Look Angelica, I don't know how to say this, but I find you very attractive and I hope you can feel the same for me." His words took her by surprise.

"Dr. Painkin I'm married."

"I know, but he doesn't deserve you. Look at yourself. You're allowing this man to take your life. You're putting your life in his hands. A man is supposed to protect his wife not beat her."

"I know. You just don't understand him. He doesn't mean to hurt me, it just happens. I'm sure at this very moment he's home sulking over it."

Dr. Painkin searched his mind for the words to help her understand what he was saying. He remembered the pact he made with the shadow figure and pressed on.

"Angelica, your husband cannot make you happy. That happiness is gone, there's nothing left but fear. You can't live a life of happiness with a heart full of fear. But I can teach you to love again, if you'll let me."

"I really appreciate the offer, but I can't leave my husband now. He needs me. All we have is each other."

"No, all he has is his self, but you can have me if you want me. Just think about it. Honey you almost died in the operating room. It was a sheer miracle that saved your life."

"I know. That's why you've got to realize that Ivan can't harm me."

"Don't you ever want to be happy?"

"I do, I just don't want to leave my husband right now. But I want you to know that I appreciate everything you've done for me. Doctor, you're a very attractive man and I'm sure that you can have any woman you want. Why are you wasting your time on me?"

He gave her no answer, kissed her hand whispering... "Think about it."

ও৲৯৶

Later that day, Ivan wondered if his wife would see him. He decided that he had better call first before she made a fool of him again. He dialed the hospital's number. A woman answered the phone and he asked for Angelica Carty's room.

"I'm sorry sir; all calls are blocked from that line. I can't put you through."

"Who made that request?"

"Her doctor did, sir. He said that the patient should not be disturbed by anyone including her spouse."

"Including her spouse?" he asked becoming hostile. "Why not? This is preposterous. You can't keep me from talking to my wife. You have no right to keep me from her. I want to talk to the doctor."

"I don't know the details sir; I can only tell you the information shown on the screen when a patient's name is activated. You will have to call administration for more details. I don't know who her doctor is."

"His name is Painkin!" He screamed. "You tell that doctor that I will not be pushed or manipulated. If it's a fight he wants, then a fight he will get."

Ivan slammed the receiver onto its bed. "I don't believe this! That doctor is trying to steal my wife. I'll kill him. How dare he think he could take my Angelica. I know he was responsible for that little act she performed the other day. She would never have done a thing like that." Ivan started thinking. He knew that if he wanted to get his wife back he would have to get that intrusive doctor out of the way. Of course with the current situation at hand, now would not be the time to draw attention.

"I'll wait until this Bob situation dies down, I can't risk going to jail now. That would be like handing my wife over to that no good doctor."

The next morning, Ivan got dressed and looked at himself in the mirror. He began talking to his reflection, rehearsing his reaction when the guys told him of his boss's death. He'd be shocked, enraged, dismayed, everything but nonchalant. He gave himself another five minutes then headed out the door. The drive to her house seemed endless. His mouth felt dry and pasty as the acid from his stomach scorched his throat. He started having anxiety attacks. What if the guys suspect me? What if they start telling the cops that I was the last one seen with her?" He thought about his discussions with the guys yesterday to see if he might have given them an indication that he was capable of killing someone. Then David popped into his mind. Telling David that he was capable of handling Bob was a direct implication that he could have killed her. Also saying that she would be meek as a lamb the next time he saw her was not good. Dead isn't considered meek, it's dead. I've got to get a grip on myself.

Ivan pulled into the driveway to Bob's house. David and Jimmy were already there. They must have just arrived because Jimmy's car door was still open. Ivan quickly fixed his composure before stepping from his car.

"What's up?"

"Nothing man, so tell us, what happened yesterday? Did Bob put the moves on you?" Jimmy asked.

"No, actually, she just wanted to discuss the receipts and welcome me to the job."

"So you're saying that she didn't try anything?"

"No. Maybe I'm not her type. What do you think? Perhaps it's that thick curly hair of yours that drew her to you. Besides, she doesn't seem to be the crew cut type!"

Jimmy frowned at him. "If she didn't get you yesterday, I bet you by the end of the week or no later than next week she'll be clawing at you."

"Man, I think you like all the action she's giving you. Paul and Robert didn't arrive I guess."

"I don't know man, they could be inside. Neither of them drives. I picked them up yesterday."

"I guess this means we can get started." Ivan rang the doorbell. He waited a couple of minutes, when he received no response, he rang it again.

"She must be here, her car's in the garage" David called after looking through the window of her garage. "Maybe she's doing one of the guys."

"You're sick Jimmy." Ivan said. "You don't give up."

"I'm telling you."

David peeped through her windows. "The lights are on in the house. Someone must be home."

Jimmy stepped up to the door and rung the bell. He held it for a while to make certain that she heard them. Still there was no answer.

"That's strange; one thing about Bob is that she demands punctuality. She can't stand for you to be late. I wonder why she isn't answering the door!" David said.

Paul and Robert had just arrived. Their wives had dropped them off this morning.

"Why are you guys congregated outside? Bob won't let you in? It's probably Ivan's fault. Did you hold out on her yesterday?" Robert said.

"Come on, cut it out, nothing happened yesterday. She just wanted to..."

Just then, Richard arrived. "What's up with Bob? I've been trying to reach her all morning and she isn't answering the phone. Her machine isn't picking up either."

"I don't know we've been trying to get in since six forty-five this morning." David responded. He looked at his watch. It was now seven thirty. Rich stepped up to her door and pulled out a set of keys. He found the key to Bob's house and opened the door.

"Barbara, are you here?" he called as he entered her foyer. Rich rested his keys on the banister, and then walked through the foyer and into the living room. She wasn't there. He checked the kitchen, she was not there either.

"Bob are you here?" he shouted again.

The guys went out back to see if perhaps she was checking on the work site but she wasn't there.

"Maybe she's upstairs sleeping or sick," David suggested. "Tell Rich to check upstairs and see if perhaps she over slept or is sick or something."

Ivan found Rich. "David suggested that perhaps you check upstairs to see if she might be up there sick or something."

Rich called out to her one last time then climbed the stairs. When he reached the top of the landing, he turned to the right where her bedroom was. He knew exactly where her room was because he had slept there on many occasions. Rich was like her right-hand man and was there for her anyway she needed him. He took care of all her banking, bills and appointments. He knew when she was fucking, who she was fucking and how long she would be fucking. He knew everything there was to know about her. She kept nothing from him. He even knew that she wanted to fuck the new guy, Ivan. She hadn't admitted it yet but he knew that it wouldn't be long before she would be showing him the perks. A big stocky fellow like that, there was no way she could pass up on that. She was definitely paying him well, one hundred thousand to start and she didn't know anything about him other than what he had on his resume. Usually, she would request a reference check but this time, she went by his looks and declared ingeniousness.

"Bob, I'm coming in. It's Richard."

He opened the door and stepped in. He saw her sprawled out on the bed, naked as a Jay bird. "Bob, the guys are waiting for you downstairs. What's wrong with you? Are you alright?"

He walked up to her and she was very pale.

"Are you sick or something?" She didn't move. He reached out to shake her when she grabbed his arm startling him. Her eyes were stretched open as far as they could possibly go without popping out of her head. Her mouth was frothy and her lips blue. She was trying to speak.

"Somebody call an ambulance, Bob's sick and I think she's dying."

Ivan and the guys hurried upstairs to see what was

going on. Richard was sitting on the bed holding Bob in his arms with the blankets wrapped around her. Ivan felt a chill as he peered over Rich's shoulder to see if Bob was alive. When he saw her lips trying to move, he backed away. Bob's eyes caught a glimpse of Ivan and she started to tremble. She was trying to speak but couldn't get enough oxygen.

"Did anyone call an ambulance?", Richard shouted.

"I did!" shouted David. They're on the way."

Just as he mentioned it, paramedics filled the room. Ivan couldn't understand why she didn't move when he shook her. He was certain that she was dead and that he had accidentally killed her. He could not let her talk, even if it meant going to the hospital and suffocating her. Killing her would not be difficult but impossible with all the doctors and paramedics around.

The paramedics tried to give her oxygen but blood shot from her mouth. She was hemorrhaging from the inside.

One of the paramedics shouted. "We got to get her to the hospital; we're going to lose her."

She went into cardiac arrest. The attendants fought to stabilize her. Her eyes rolled to the back of her head.

"Let's get her out of here." The paramedic insisted.

They rushed her downstairs and out to the ambulance. She was rushed to the nearest hospital which was only five minutes away. She was rushed into the trauma room. She tried to pull the doctor down to her lips so that she could, even in death, have victory over Ivan for what he had done to her. It wasn't bad enough that he tried to choke her to death, and then drown her in the bath tub, not to mention scrapping her intestine wall while trying to clean her up and finally humiliating her by having some strange man rape her while she was trying to die peacefully.

The doctor fought to control her by holding her down thinking that she would lock onto him in death but she was actually trying to communicate with him.

"Clear." Bob felt a bolt of electricity shoot through her. That was all she needed, her life escaped that very instant. The doctor looked at the screen. There was nothing but a flat line.

"Clear," he shouted again but his efforts were futile for the woman that he was trying to save had died and there was nothing anyone could do to save her life. Her assailant would go free because her testimony died with her.

"Okay, the time of death is eight-thirty. Let's get this body to the morgue. Somebody get a hold of her family."

Richard was pacing the hospital floor waiting for the word on Bob's condition. When he spotted the doctor, he hurried over to him but could see the doctor shaking his head negatively as he neared him.

"I'm sorry, we lost her. There was nothing we could do. It was just a matter of time before she died."

"Did she say anything?"

"No, she was so hysterical that we had a hard time getting the equipment hooked up to her."

"She didn't try to say anything?"

"No, she was just fighting for her life."

"What happened to her?"

"We don't know yet, are you her husband?"

"No, she didn't have a husband; I'm her friend and the one responsible for her estate."

"Are there any members of her family that can be contacted to claim the body?"

"I'm all she has. I have a signed proxy to speak on

her behalf. Anything you need to ask, I can answer it." Richard explained. He wiped his eyes, fighting to control his display of hurt. "I want an autopsy done. I want to know what happened to her. Right away!" Richard demanded with a quivering voice.

"Well, give your name and number to the nurse and she'll have pathology contact you as soon as we know something."

Richard took childlike steps to the nurses' station. His feet felt heavy.

She was so vibrant and full of life, he reminisced. How could she just die like that? Something had to have happened. There was no way that Bob could have been sick and he not know about it. The nurse could see that the man was in shock.

"Is there anything I can do?" the nurse asked him.

He broke down in tears. She rushed around the counter and wrapped her arms around him. He welcomed the comfort of her arms because he knew that he would never see the woman he loved again. When he finally got control of himself, the nurse took the information from him and told him that someone would be calling him.

When Richard got back to Bob's house, Ivan and the other guys were waiting to hear the news. They had been talking about the scene they'd just witnessed when Richard walked in.

"So is she alright?" Ivan asked trying to see if she might have said anything to Richard.

"No, she died."

Ivan's expression changed from concern to sorrow. "Wow, such a nice beautiful woman. Was she sick or something?"

"No, not to my knowledge, she was trying to say something but she never got a chance to get it out. Of course, when the results come back from pathology, we will at least know the cause of death."

"This must be hard for you. You two were very close huh?" Robert asked.

"Yeah, I really am going to miss her."

"Well, I guess this is it for us?" Paul questioned.

"No, I want the job that Bob wanted done to this house carried out. Ivan you will still be in charge and I want you guys to work as though she was still here. I will not let her dreams die. If you guys can carry that out, I will make certain that you always have a job with this company."

"But wasn't Bob the President of the company?"

"Yes, but she left the company to me. She said that if anything ever happened to her that she wanted me to take over as long as I promised to carry out her wishes."

"Alright, then can we meet back here tomorrow, I don't think that I can work today after all that's happened."

"Sure. You guys take the rest of the week off. I'll see you back here on Monday."

"You'll let us know if we can be of help won't you?" Ivan asked.

"Yes, thanks for asking." The guys left the house in a single file line. Not another word was exchanged. No one wanted to disturb the solemn aura that they were each filled with that very moment. Of course, Ivan knew that he had victory over her because she didn't have the chance to tell what happened.

CHAPTER

5

Angelica has been in the hospital for two weeks now. Her recovery was nothing shy of remarkable and beyond belief. The x-rays showed no sign of trauma. It was as though the incident never occurred. Although she had been advised by her doctor not to get up from her bed, she looked into her cabinet and found a pair of slippers made of paper. She sat up, slid them onto her feet and motioned to stand up. At first she was off balance because she hadn't stood in awhile but that only lasted a couple of moments. When the sudden shock of standing passed, she took slow, easy steps to the bathroom. When she reached the bathroom, Angelica looked at her reflection. Everything was back to normal with the exception of her bruised eye. She didn't imagine that it would ever go back to normal since she had been hit in it so many times. The doctor had just removed her bandages only a day ago. He told her that she needed to remain in the hospital for at least six weeks so that he could make certain that her body had enough time to heal itself. Dr. Painkin also recommended that she consider leaving her husband. As much as she wanted to, she knew she never could. Ivan would kill her first.

Angelica thought back to the doctor's words. The next time you may not get a second chance. Someone or something wanted you to live and you should take advantage of that. Live Angelica, live. She heard the doctor's words echoing. She wanted to live a peaceful life but sometimes when you make bad choices in life, you just have to live with them.

She turned on the water in the shower stall and waited a moment to give it time to reach the perfect temperature. When she saw the steam on the door, she knew that it was ready. She untied her gown, letting it fall to the floor, and then stepped into the shower. She let the water fall onto her shoulders and down her breasts and back. It felt so good to take a shower again. For a week and a half, she had been sponge bathed by nurses. Finally three days ago, they decided that she could handle that job herself. She lathered her cloth and rubbed it all over her body letting the fresh smell of Ivory fill the air. Something tingled inside her as she thought of Dr. Painkin's touch. He held her hand so gently when he spoke to her. He was nothing like Ivan; demanding all the time. Dr. Painkin would be gentle and sweet. He would be attentive to her physical needs and not rush their passion. If he came in this very moment, she would make love to him. She let her hands glide over her torso while thinking of him, down to her...she heard someone knocking at the door. Angelica paused for a moment to make certain that she actually heard the door when it opened. Someone stepped in.

"Angelica, are you alright?" the voice called out to her.

She opened the door a crack and it was her doctor. He was standing just inside the bathroom with his back turned to her. He wasn't in the white smock she usually saw him in. He was dressed in civilian clothing. He was wearing a pair of khaki Dockers with a cotton shirt and loafer shoes. His body appeared muscular. He had broad shoulders and his waist narrowed at the hip. He was well built and sexier than she imagined.

"I just stopped by to see how you were doing before I left for the night."

His back was still turned to her.

"Oh thank you," she said while blushing. "I appreciate that."

"Listen, I'm sorry if I offended you yesterday. It's just that I hate to see a woman being abused by a man especially someone as beautiful as yourself. Hey, I'll talk to you another time because I don't want to make you uncomfortable or anything. When I didn't see you in your bed, I thought that something might have happened to you since you weren't supposed to be out of bed in the first place."

"I know, I just felt dirty and needed to take a shower."

"Are you all right in there? How does your head feel?"

"It feels fine. When I first stood up, it felt a little woozy but that cleared up pretty quickly."

"Well listen, I didn't mean to impose on you so I'll just wait for you outside. The last thing I would want is to make you feel uncomfortable."

"No, no, you're not making me uncomfortable at all, in fact I'm kind of glad you're here, I needed a little company."

Finding her statement strange, he pressed a little further.

"Is there something wrong or on your mind?"

"No, I just wanted someone to be here with me."

"Would you like for me to wait for you outside? I'll call Nurse Green."

"No, please stay here, right where you are."

The doctor felt confused, he didn't know what angle she was coming from. Had she decided to take him up on his offer? Was there something she wanted him to see? Was she afraid of something or someone? What would make her want him stay in the bathroom with her.

"Angelica, are you sure there's nothing wrong?"

"I'm sure doc, everything's perfect. I just want you to stay here with me."

"Why don't I call the nurse in for you? Do you need help with anything?"

"No, please just stay there."

She let the water rinse the last bit of lather from her body then stepped out of the stall.

"Can you pass me that towel?"

Dr. Painkin picked up the towel and passed it back to her without turning around.

"I'm over here," she laughed at his poor attempt to avoid looking at her. "It's been a long time since some-one made love to me. Will you make love to me doc?"

Her words took him by surprise. Although he imagined her saying those same words, somehow he felt that he should be running away from her. Yet there was something in him that made him stay.

"Doesn't your husband make love to you?"

"No, my husband fucks me," she frankly told him. "Ivan doesn't know how to make love to a woman. I'm not saying that it isn't pleasurable because it is, but I want someone to show me a little tenderness. I want you to love me with the same smoothness you had in your voice when you told me that you had feelings for me. Can you do that?"

Without thinking he answered.

"Yes." He turned around and looked at her. She stood before him, watching him with her hair slick from the water with little droplets cascading down her breasts like icing on a cake. Her olive skin was beautiful with peach undertones. Her legs were shapely and short, her body petite in size. She was like a cute little Barbie doll. He stood there observing her assets before stepping up close to her. He pulled her face up to meet his lips and tenderly kissed her. Her mouth opened to welcome him. He made slow sweet sweeps across her mouth with his tongue. His hands massaged her back gently while she wrestled with his zipper. He wanted to stop this because he knew that it wasn't right. This was not the time or place but he knew that if he stopped it now, he may never get the chance again. She would probably feel embarrassed and not speak to him again so he continued to allow her seduction to go on. He lowered his lips to her neck then down to her erect nipple. Taking it into his mouth, he began encircling it with his tongue then gently sucking it and letting it go. She let out a moan.

"Doc that feels so good."

"Call me Steve."

"Steve that feels so good."

He kissed her belly moving downward.

"Steve what are you doing?"

"I'm going to thoroughly make love to you. Isn't that what you wanted?"

"Yes but."

Steve cut her off mid sentence.

"You mean to tell me your husband never went down on you?"

"No. He'd never do anything like that."

"Has anyone been down on you?"

"Ivan was my first and only until now!" His eyes met hers. He wondered how such a delicate flower could be mistreated so badly. She had been deprived the beauty of lovemaking.

"Trust me; it is something you will never forget. In

fact, you may never want anything else after."

He sat her on the counter and opened her legs. Her sweet aroma still lingered behind the fragrance of the soap. The aphrodisiac he loved so well. He allowed his tongue to open her lips with a little help from his fingers. He could feel her thighs tightening around his head.

"Don't fight it baby, enjoy it."

Angelica felt a fire she had never known before. Her body began to move against his face as his tongue entered her.

"Oh God!" she cried, catching hold of her mouth after realizing that her outcry was too loud.

"You like that baby? You like that? Come to papa."

When his tongue struck the right cord, her body thrust against his face. She fought to feel his tongue inside her. He pushed his tongue into her but the flames of her ardor were insatiable.

"Give it to me!" she demanded. He stood up in a flash and worked his way into her. Her body began to tremble. He started with easy, gentle strokes but soon realized that she wanted him to be rough. He pulled her to the edge of the counter and held her thighs up forcing her to lean against the mirror. When he reached the right angle her climax was met. When he felt himself beginning to ejaculate, he pulled out of her because he knew that was the last thing he needed to do at this point. That would have been a definite mistake.

Steve stood there between her legs with his arms wrapped around her searching her eyes for emotions. "Angelica, are you still okay with this?"

"Yes, doctor, I'm fine now. You have cured me."

Steve looked at her wondering how he should take that. He wondered if this would be the end.

"So what happens now?"

"I don't know."

"Well how do you feel? Are you happy? Disappointed? What do you want to happen now? The ball is in your court."

"Steve, believe me, I would love to take you up on your offer but you and I both know that Ivan will not let me just walk away from our marriage. Our vows were till death do us part and trust me, he'd kill me before he'd let me leave, especially if it's with you."

"If you want, we can have him arrested."

"Arrested? You mean put in jail? I can't do that to him!"

"What do you mean you can't do that to him? What about what he did to you. I don't know if you know this but your recovery is purely a miracle. I have performed many operations and no one who is wheeled into the operating room with your type of injuries survives. According to medical data, you should be dead right now but something wanted you to live."

"You're just an excellent doctor."

"No, Angelica that was a miracle that happened in that operating room. You were meant to live honey. My recommendation to you would be to let that man go and have him locked up because you may not walk away the next time."

"Ivan wouldn't kill me."

"Maybe not intentionally, but with his anger being what it is, he may really hurt you the next time. I for one don't want to see that happen. I couldn't bare the thought of knowing he might have the opportunity to hurt you again. Please say you'll come with me. Come live with me. You don't have to go back to him."

She allowed her eyes to escape his and wonder aimlessly at the walls until they finally rested on the floor.

"I just don't know if there is any where I can hide from him."

"Listen, I'll sign you out and take you to another facility where he can't find you and I will personally see to it that you are taken care of. He doesn't even have to know that you're gone. I can have the staff tell him when he calls that you left the hospital and gave no information or indication where you were going. How does that sound?"

"I don't know. Ivan won't settle for that, I'm sure that he must still be angry with me because of the way I treated him the other day when I asked him to leave. I haven't heard from him since. He hasn't even called."

"I know. I had your calls blocked so that he wouldn't be able to call and your visitor's passes were pulled so that no one could visit."

"Wait, what about my mother? No one has told her that I'm in here. She would have come by now."

"Listen, we can contact your mother when I have you placed in another facility. What do you think about that?" He lifted her chin so that her eyes would meet his. "I'm trying to save your life. That husband of yours is dangerous. He isn't good for you or anyone else for that matter. You had better let him go before it's too late."

"All right, I'll go with you. But you must promise to let me call my mother as soon as we find someplace else. You promise?" She waited for his response with her grey eyes intently on his.

"I promise."

He led her back into the shower stall and while she showered away the dew of their lovemaking. While she covered her body with soap his watchful eyes absorbed her tantalizing movements. When she prepared to lather up her private part, he stopped her.

"Let me do that for you." He allowed his hands to cleanse her while pleasing her with his fingers. His lips met hers in a deep meaningful kiss while their tongues danced wildly. He pulled her hand so that she could massage his erection. Her lather filled hand smoothly caressed him until he spilled onto the floor. Steve continued kissing her, feeling her, touching her rendering her helplessly craving the culmination of passion which was reaching the peak of explosion.

"Mrs. Carty are you alright?" the nurse called to her while knocking on the bathroom door. "I'm here to check your vital signs for the night, will you be out soon?"

"Ah, yes Nurse Green, I'll be out in a moment."

"Listen, your chart says that you are not supposed to be out of the bed, not even to go to the bathroom."

"I know, but I really needed to come in here."

"Well listen, I have to check your signs so that I can leave. I have already done everyone else. You are the last patient on my list and you are not about to hold me up young lady."

She opened the door to find a pile of civilian clothes on the floor. Were you going somewhere Ms. Carty? I see that you have some clothes..." Her voice changed as she began to examine the contents on the floor. She noticed that the clothing were men's clothes. Then she saw two shadows through the shower door.

"Who's in there with you Mrs. Carty? That isn't allowed in the hospital. Besides that, visiting hours are over."

Angelica's heart was racing while she stood pressed against her doctor's chest. She was hoping that the nosy nurse would at least have the decency to leave the room and allow her to get dressed.

"I'll be out in a minute Nurse Green. Could you

please wait outside?"

"Just hurry up!" Dr. Painkin was hoping that he didn't leave his tag on his clothes at least not in a way that it could be seen. He waited for the nurse to leave the bathroom before he came out. He blotted himself dry and told Angelica that he would go out through the other door so that the nurse wouldn't see him then come into her room after the nurse took her vital signs and left for the night. Then the door opened.

"Oh by the way Mrs. Carty, your husband is in the room waiting to see you." Then whispering... "Dr. Painkin, you had better get dressed quickly and exit through the next room. You know you aren't supposed to be fucking the patients anyway, especially the married ones."

Embarrassed, he hurried through the adjoining room. Angelica put on a clean gown and robe then returned to her bed where her husband was sitting waiting patiently for her to come out.

"Angelica, before you call security on me, I want to say that I both love and miss you very much. I hope that you can forgive me for the pain and suffering I have put you through. I was wrong and hope that you can eventually find it in your heart to forgive me."

He looked deep into her eyes searching for just a glimpse of forgiveness; instead he saw shock, surprise, deceit and knew that she was hiding something from him.

"Ivan, this is not a good time for me and I really don't want to see you."

Something was going on and she was not doing a good job of hiding it. He could see right through her. There was definitely something going on between her and the doctor. Either he has already told her that he's interested in her and she's considering it or she's fucking him. Ivan knew that it was one or the other and he was going to get to the bottom of it.

"So what's the good doctor saying? Are you coming along alright? How long does he expect you to have to stay in here?"

"Probably another four weeks."

"Four more weeks huh? What then. Any home treatments?"

Angelica looked at him in dismay wondering if he was trying to insinuate that she and the doctor was having an affair.

"No, he didn't say that I would require therapy after release. But I would imagine that I would have to have follow-up exams."

Ivan curled his index finger beneath his chin as though he was thinking.

"I see, so you're already anticipating the need to see the good doctor when you get out of here?"

"What are you trying to say Ivan?" she blurted out angrily.

"What I'm saying is that my wife is being seduced by the one I hired to take care of her. I'm paying his salary honey and it's not to fuck my wife. You two think you're pulling wool over my head but you're not. I'm not blind and I know when someone is interested in my wife. You tell that doctor that if he continues to get in my way or try to prevent me from seeing you, that I will kill him! Do you hear me?"

Angelica's heart raced with fear. If he continued at the pace he was going, he would definitely strike her. His eyes were showing that violent anger that always manifests itself just before he begins his rage. She reached for her buzzer but he grabbed her hand.

"You don't have to do that honey, I'm leaving now, I told you that I have no intention of hurting you again.

I want to love you, not hurt you. But as you can see, you have made me very angry and I must go now before you cause me to do something that we will both regret."

He kissed her hand lightly then her forehead and turned to leave the room. Remembering that he had something for her, he turned around and walked over to her bed. Angelica cringed, fearing that he was going to strike her after all, but when he reached down at the foot of the bed and lifted a large pink teddy bear holding a heart which read "I Love You." She realized that he was not going to hit her. He handed it to her then bent down to whisper in her ear that he loved her and wouldn't let anyone or anything come between them, not even death.

He walked out of the room and down the corridor. While walking, he felt a sense of security because he knew that Dr. Painkin didn't stand a chance with her now. There was no way she would attempt to leave him. Although he wanted to rebuild her confidence in him, and resented the fact that he had to scare her like that, but he had no other choice, if he allowed time to go by, the doctor would have cut off all his connections with her. It was bad enough he had to raise hell just to see her. No calls were being transferred to her room and no visitors allowed, who does Dr. Painkin think he is? Trying to come between him and his wife!

He walked passed the nurses station hoping to catch a glimpse of the doctor. He didn't see him anywhere so he left the hospital and found his car. He looked at his watch; the time read eight o'clock. Tomorrow would be another long eventful day so he decided that he would go home and get some rest. During his drive home, he wondered how Bob survived him strangling her just to die the next day in front of him and his crew. He guessed she was still fighting to tell somebody. Didn't she know that some things were meant to be left unsaid? He smiled to himself to think that he still got away with it, not to mention, she was a great piece of ass.

๛

Dr. Painkin returned to Angelica's room. She was laying there holding the teddy her husband brought to her.

"Are you alright?"

"Yes, I'm fine."

"You don't look fine; did your husband do anything to hurt you?"

"No, he just reminded me of something that I already knew."

"What's that?"

"That he has no intention of letting me go, even if it means killing me, I mean you."

The doctor had a shocked look on his face. He thought for a moment before answering.

"Angel, I hope you don't mind if I call you that because that's what I see when I look at you. I'm not afraid of your husband and I won't mind killing him if it comes to that as long as I know that you will be on my side." He waited for a response. When he received none, he continued. "Are you still willing to leave with me? I will move you tonight."

"Steve, I don't think that this is a good idea, what if we get hurt or something happens?"

"Nothing will happen, trust me."

His eyes pleaded with her. He would by no means allow that man to hurt her, not in his presence. Angelica searched her heart for direction. She wanted to start over again but feared what would happen if she walked away.

"Angel, sometimes you just have to take a chance

and hope for the best. Come with me."

He held her hand waiting for a response. She pulled her hand away from him, opened the draw next to her showing him that she didn't have any clothes here. The doctor went out and returned with some clothes. It was a pair of blue jeans and a red sweater which belonged to Nurse Green. She put them on without question and he handed her his trench coat and told her to put it on. The doctor watched her, surprised yet happy because he knew that she was taking a chance. He had no intentions of letting her down. He would protect her even if it meant his life.

He told her to wait for him to return. He went to the nurses' station and requested discharge papers. He returned to the room with the papers for Angelica to sign. She quickly looked over the notes, signed it and gave it back to him. She hoped that she made the right choice and wasn't signing her death warrant. Painkin took it to the nurses' station.

Nurse Green caught hold of his arm and pulled him off to the side out of earshot.

"What do you think you're doing Steve?" She asked with her hand on her hip.

"I'm saving that woman's life."

"You're stealing that man's wife is what you're doing and if you're not careful."

"He doesn't deserve her." Steve blurted out.

"I know but this isn't the way to correct it."

"This isn't just about protecting her, I have feelings for her. I care about her."

"Dr. Painkin, I don't think you're making a rational decision. What about your career? Think about that. Let God help her."

"He did already and he told me to take care of her. Look, this is the only way I know right now and it feels right. So to me it can't be wrong. So give me your blessings and remember what I told you to tell him when he visits again."

"I know, I'll put it into her chart that she discharged herself and walked out of the hospital. I'll make certain that there is no indication that you had anything to do with it. I'll tell him that she left right after him."

"Good, that way he'll realize that she was attempting to leave him and will leave her alone."

"What are you going to do with her?"

"The less you know, the better off you'll be. He can't get out of you what you don't know. Okay?"

"Okay, but you be careful and make certain that she's taken care of."

Dr. Painkin returned to Angelica's room.

"Are you ready?"

"No, but let's go anyway."

He led her out of the hospital through the private parking lot provided for employee's use. He helped her into his Infinity Q45 then got in on the driver's side. He made certain that her seat belt was fastened before starting the car. He put his Four Play CD into the player and soft jazz filled the car.

Angelica felt so comfortable with him although she wondered whether Ivan would jump out from some hiding place in a crazed fury but he didn't. The drive to Steve's house was nice and quiet. He must have sensed her fear because he squeezed her hand to reassure her. He didn't start a conversation because he wanted her to relax and enjoy the music. His gold Infinity glided across the road as though the streets were perfect. The night lay still and quiet and not a sound from the outside penetrated the orchestra which serenaded them.

After awhile, Angelica felt comfortable although she treaded on ground to which she was unfamiliar, she found herself falling asleep. The drive home seemed extra long because Steve was taking someone's life on an uncertain journey. Even though it was scary it still seemed right. Finally, he pulled in front of his cozy little home. The night's light shone on the stone front of his house and the fountain appeared to have crystals flowing into its pool. He touched Angelica's arm.

"Darling we're here."

She opened her eyes looking through the windshield at the house before her. She was in heaven. The house appeared peaceful; somewhere she could find rest from the cares of the world.

"So do you like it?"

"It's magnificent. You live alone?"

"Yes. Just me, well actually, I have a Persian cat who resides with me. Her name is Sandy. Of course, I don't see that being a problem. I already told her that someone would be joining us soon so she would become second in my life."

Angelica gave him a smile and opened her door. She walked up to the fountain observing its beauty.

"This is a beautiful statue. I don't believe I've ever seen anything like it."

"Yeah she's very special to me."

"Did you know her? Your statement sounded personal."

"She was my mother. She died at the hands of an abusive husband."

"Oh I'm sorry. That must have been really difficult for you."

"Many times she would say that she was going to leave him but for some reason, she remained with him until one day he came in drunk and beat her to death.

She came into the hospital with conditions similar to your own; the only difference is that she wasn't given another chance. Angelica, you've got to realize that your husband won't change. No one who beats a woman should be given another chance."

Angelica was speechless. She saw the hurt deep in the abyss of his pupils.

"You remind me of my mother. She was sweet, gentle and forgiving like you. There was always a silver lining in every cloud. Everyone deserved a second chance."

"That's beautiful Steve. It's not wrong to hope for the best, sometimes things just don't work out the way you hoped it would."

"I know. I can appreciate how you feel. Come on let's go in. I'm sure you want to get settled in. We can talk as much as you like when we get inside."

He opened his garage door.

"Give me a moment while I put the car in the garage."

After he had parked the car, he returned to her side. He waited a moment to see that the door closed to the garage properly then put his key into the lock to open the door. He led her in and showed her around the house. They sat out on the veranda and watched the starry sky without saying a word, both wondering if the right choice had been made.

CHAPTER
6

Ivan looked at his clock to check the time. It was five minutes past five o'clock. He reached over to the pillow next to him remembering that his wife was still in the hospital. He had dreamt that she had come home and things were back to normal. He laid there a moment hesitating before he got up to get ready for work. He found his work clothes and placed them on a chair next to the bathroom door. He took a nice long shower, shaved and got dressed. He wondered what the day would be like now that Bob wouldn't be there and Rich would be handling things. Of course, it did strike him funny that Bob wasn't dead when he left her but he just shrugged and figured that she was just stronger than what he had anticipated. She had a will to live but it just wasn't strong enough. He checked himself one more time in the mirror and went to the kitchen.

He checked the refrigerator; there was nothing there but a quart of milk on the verge of spoiling, one egg and a frozen TV dinner in the freezer.

"I guess its muffin day. I'll stop at Seven Eleven on the way." He threw up his hands indicating that he was failing at this homemaking thing. He grabbed his jacket and headed out the door.

He pulled in front of the Seven Eleven store, parked his car and hurried inside to pick up his muffin. At the counter, the attendant was giving him the eye. He wondered what it was about women that angered him the most. The fact that they couldn't stand to see a good looking man pass by without wanting him or the fact that they felt they had to have him no matter what.

"Hi big fellow, I haven't see you around here before."

"Yeah, well maybe you haven't been looking hard enough. I practically come here everyday with the exception of weekends."

"Hmmm... I'm sure that if you had been here before I would have noticed you, but anyway, my name's Geneva."

"Hello Geneva. I believe I like that name."

"Thanks. Say, how about you and I get together sometime?"

"No, I don't think that would be a good idea."

"Why are you married or something?"

"Yes, as a matter of fact I am." He said holding up his ring finger. The gold band sparked.

"That woman must be pretty lucky to have a dedicated man like yourself. Especially with you being handsome and all."

"Thank you, I'd take that as a compliment."

"So there's no chance of us getting together."

Ivan cast a grin her way and paid for his muffin and coffee.

"See you tomorrow," she called out to him as left the store.

"Take care Geneva."

She smiled because she knew that he'd be back and she would be his at least once. She watched his big tight buns strut. He shifted his large shoulders as he walked and she could tell that beneath that jacket was a man with guns the size of a bowling ball and in his pants, a staff the size of a Parks Sausage roll.

Ivan returned to his car and checked his watch. It was ten to seven. He had to hurry to work. In five minutes, he pulled in front of Bob's house. Rich had just arrived as well.

"What's up, Ivan. You got here just in time." Rich got out of his car looking around and saw that the other guys were already there ready to work. They stood there waiting for him to open the door and let them in. Of course, Rich was a harder person to work with. They were hoping that they would be able to continue working under Ivan's supervision without Rich's interjections. He managed the office well but as far as physical work was concerned, he hadn't a clue but his ego made him crave control and now that he had it, the terror began.

Rich opened the door and held it open so that the guys could enter and right away he started giving orders. Ivan stood back and listened. You could tell by the sneer on his face that he did not agree with the instructions given by Rich. When he could take no more, he protested...

"Rich I think that things would move a great deal smoother if you allowed me to carry out Bob's requests. She did leave me in charge of the work and definitely felt that I was more than qualified for the job. I'm not trying to undermine you but I had already received direction and the guys have already been prepped so there is no need in you changing things."

Rich's face was turning a new shade of red. The guys could tell that Ivan took him by surprise and it wasn't a surprise he appreciated.

"So, you believe that you can handle the job better than I can. What makes you feel you are so qualified for the job?"

"Well for one thing, I was hired and certainly if not

you, Bob thought I was qualified for the job not to mention she gave me access to any funds needed to complete the job. More over she gave me hire and fire privileges. Must I go on?"

"No, you need not go on. Bob is dead now and her judgment no longer stands so things will be run my way or no way. Do you understand that?"

He focused his piercing eyes on Ivan as to say I don't want to have to say this again. Then he turned to the other guys.

"Is there anyone else here that feels that I am not qualified to handle this job?"

All the guys looked at each other to see if there was one who had the guts to tell this man that he definitely belonged in an office and not in the field. "Good, I presume that your silence meant that we are all in agreement."

Then David answered.

"Well sir, I feel that Ivan would do a much better job. He was hired to do the job and so far has made a good start so needless to say, I think that you should let your pride go and allow him to do the job for which he was hired to do."

Rich looked at the rest of the guys and could see that even though their mouths didn't openly confess their opinions they all felt the same way.

"Ivan, David I really don't like what I see happening here but I feel that perhaps I will allow things to continue the way they were originally planned but the first sign of it not being done properly, I will terminate you. All of you!" He walked out of the door and told them that he would be returning at five o'clock to check on their work and to make certain that things were moving along smoothly.

When he was gone, they guys mimicked him.

Shadow Lover 69

"If things aren't going smoothly, I'll terminate you. All of you." David started.

Jimmy the quiet one of the group, was standing there posed like a faggot with his hands on his hips and his hand pointing at the other guys with his wrist hanging down. They laughed at him mocking their boss.

"You shouldn't make fun of the man paying your salary you know Jimmy!" David said.

"Okay guys lets get to work before Mr. Boss Man returns." Ivan instructed.

They followed him to the rear of her house to where the pool was. Even though it was the early Spring, the day was chillier than usual. So the work took more effort than needed. In fact, judging by the clouds, it appeared to want to rain any moment. Of course it didn't, but just the idea that it could, made it worse.

Ivan and the guys spent the day clearing the pool site of any debris from the ground. The cement had probably arrived over the weekend. Ivan instructed Paul to start the cement mixer since that was his specialty. He knew how to whip that stuff in two shakes of a lamb's tail and never did it have to be done twice. In the meantime, Jimmy and Ivan worked on the coating of the sides so that the bottom of the pool could be covered with cement. That was Robert and Paul's job. When they were pleased with the job, they summoned Ivan to take a look at it for approval. He found that it was level and no rough spots were seen, he looked at his watch.

"I guess Rich should be showing up soon. Let's get cleaned up so that we can be prepared to leave. I want everyone ready to leave when he gets here. There should be nothing for him to do other than inspect the premises.

"So fellows, I can see that you cleaned up before I got here. How much have you accomplished today?" Rich said turning his attention to Ivan who was standing next to the pool waiting for inspection. He walked over to Rich prepared to give him a report.

"We've completed the ground work today. I presume that I don't have to give you details of that because you are proficient in this. So take a look and we will get out of here as it is our time to leave and there is nothing else that can be completed in such little time." He waited for Rich's protest but received none. He seemed to be preoccupied with something to have care or concern about his smart remark.

As the guys were preparing to leave the house, the police showed up at the door.

"I need to speak to Mr. Richard Davis." The officer said showing his badge.

David examined the badge and called Richard. He came to the door.

"Hi, I'm Richard Davis what can I do for you?"

"The hospital records indicated that you were the one to find Barbara Givens before she died, is this information correct?"

"Yes, as soon as I discovered her, I made certain that she was taken directly to the hospital. In fact, she was taken by the ambulance which arrived promptly."

"Do you have any idea what happened to her before you arrived?"

"No. The guys here were waiting for her to let them in so that the work she hired them to do on her house could start. I had tried to reach her all morning because we had an important client calling with an urgent situation and when I received no response, I decided that I'd better get over here just in case for some reason she over slept. When I got here, all the guys were standing outside waiting for her to open the door."

"So how is it that you were able to enter her house and find her?"

"I have the keys to her house. I am her business partner and a very close friend of hers. In fact, I have access to all of her records. She corresponded with me with everything she did."

"I see. Were you intimate with Ms. Davis?"

"Occasionally. Why?"

"Did you know that she had multiple lovers?"

"Why are you questioning me like this? What does any of this have to do with Bob's death?"

"Well forensics show that she was murdered. Someone had kicked the living shit out of her, rupturing her spleen. Her whole insides were damaged. The surface remained in tact but who ever did this meant for it not to be visible. She was tortured."

"I see. I presume that you're blaming me for that?"

"No sir. My job is to bring you in for questioning because you are the primary suspect since you are the only one who has something to gain."

"Well, I'm sure that she probably gained a great deal of enemies in her line of work."

"What ever the case, we have to take you in."

"What if I refuse? I have rights you know!"

"Then get ready for a serious beat down. Walk or crawl you're coming with us. We have a warrant for your arrest. So I suggest you come quietly and forget about those TV crime shows, they'll get you killed."

The guys stood around listening. This was all too surprising to them. As spineless as Rich has been, none of them could see him doing anything as violent as that.

"Hey listen, Rich, you'd better go with them. Don't make a scene. They'll see that this has all been a terrible mistake. The way you're behaving will only build their suspicion," Ivan said. He assured Richard that he should just cooperate and go down for questioning. "They will probably let you go shortly after. It's just that you're the first up for questioning because of your relationship with Bob. It would only be right to start with the one who has the most to gain. We'll see you tomorrow bright and early for work."

The officers motioned for Rich to follow them. They allowed him to lock the door then put the handcuffs on Rich and escorted him to the squad car to go to the precinct. Ivan and the others watched their boss be taken away like a common criminal. None of them believed him to be capable of a violent act especially since his relationship with Bob was so close. Only time will tell.

CHAPTER
7

Early the next morning Angelica woke up to find that she was not in the hospital bed where she had been for the past two weeks. She was laying in a cloud of feathers covered with royal blue satin. She hadn't had a comfortable sleep like that in a long time. The bed was so soft and filled with the smell of lavender. She had dreamt that Dr. Painkin had swept her off her feet and taken her away from the clutches of her mean husband to live the rest of their lives together in happiness. Of course the last thing she remembered in reality was sitting on a veranda with him staring out at the starry night's sky. How did she get into this bed?

She sat up and placed her feet in a pair of male wool slippers. They were by far too big for her but it covered her feet so that she wouldn't have to walk barefoot through the house. In the next room, she heard someone talking. She cracked the door and saw Dr. Painkin sitting at a desk speaking with someone on the phone. She listened by the door.

❧

"So when can I bring her by? Tomorrow would be great. I really need you to take special care of her and there are to be no visitors unless I approve it first. No one is to know of her. I want her to be registered under the name of Regina Weston. No, this is important. There is nothing illegal going on. I'm just trying to save this woman's life. Can you understand that? Alright alright, I'll tell you what's going on. This woman came into my hospital suffering from an acute hematoma which was due to a severe beating. Yes her husband was beating her. We were able to take care of it but I don't want her to go back to her husband. No, he doesn't know that she's going to be placed in your facility that's why I'm registering her under a different name. I'm doing it because I love her! Thanks friend. I knew that I could count on you. He hung up the phone and turned around to see Angelica standing at the door.

"Good morning darling, I didn't know you were up. Did you sleep well last night?"

"Yes, thank you."

"What's wrong? You don't seem happy. Is there something on your mind you want to discuss?" He waited for her to respond.

"Dr. Painkin..."

"Steve," he cut her off.

"Steve, why am I so special to you? I'm sure there are plenty of women out there that would be more deserving of your love and kindness than me."

"No, there's something special about you Angel. I don't quite know what it is but there's something inside me that tells me that we were meant to be together."

"I don't understand, we only met two weeks ago when my husband brought me to the hospital."

"I know. I can't explain it but during surgery, there was someone else there who touched me and caused me to know how to save your life. From that moment on I was in love with you. Something started stirring in me which let me know that you and I are meant for each other. At first, I didn't think anything of it, but who ever it was, followed me into the lavatory, then left. There is something special about you Angelica; I don't know what it is but I believe that it is at the very least my destiny to protect you."

Angelica listened to what the doctor was saying. Although it sounded preposterous, she believed him because never in a million years would she allow someone to kidnap her from the hospital and bring her to their house when she had no prior acquaintance.

"Okay, let's say that what you're saying is true, what happens when my husband finds out that I'm no longer at the hospital?"

He walked over to her and kissed her on the forehead.

"Let me worry about that when the time comes."

"You don't understand. He's not going to buy that I just left; he will find a way to check the entire hospital to see if my room was changed. He's not going to give up without a fight."

"Angelica, I assure you that nothing is going to happen to you. Somehow I believe that and you're just going to have to trust me. Can you do that?"

She paused a moment.

"Okay, I guess so."

He held her hands then pulled her close to him. She hadn't felt safe in a long time. Now she was being loved by a man she hardly knew. Steve felt a growing desire for her and desperately wanted to make love to her. However, he realized that he would have to control those urges because he didn't want to taint her impression of him and cause her to think that all he wanted from her was sex. He would wait, when she wanted it, she'll take it, just like she did in the hospital. Soon, he hoped because he was ready to burst.

He escorted her downstairs to the sitting room. She sat down on his plush sofa with her knee in the chair so that she could face him.

"So tell me about yourself, your parents, how you met your husband and what made you marry him."

"Well, I grew up in a small town in North Carolina with my parents, where everything was slow and simple. It didn't take a rocket scientist to figure out what made the world turn. My parents were farmers, pretty good farmers I might add, but I knew that wasn't the life I wanted to lead. When I would look up at the sky and see how infinite it was, I realized that there was a world outside of the one I knew and I wanted to explore it. Of course, I never had the guts to leave and do things on my own. None of my girlfriends were willing to take a chance. So that's when I met Ivan. I was only twenty-one then. He was a New Yorker, a City Slicker. He used to come by and take me out to dinner, show me nice places and buy me nice things. Now don't get me wrong, these things were always there its just that I didn't have anyone to take me to them. I fell in love with him because he was so mysterious, so outgoing, courageous, all the things I wanted in a man. One year during homecoming, he showed up with an engagement ring. I was so ecstatic that I wouldn't hear anything my parents had to say about him. Everything they mentioned to me, I already knew. I knew that he was fifteen years older than me, more experienced in life, but who gave a damn. I was going to leave this tiny, little five-thousand people population town and move to the larger cities in North Carolina where things moved faster and life became more uncertain. At first, we lived in Elizabeth City, and then we moved to Fayetteville. Finally, he decided that he wanted to leave North Carolina completely so we moved here to New York. I couldn't believe it, things moved extremely fast here. Tall buildings and everything was here. We have buildings in North Carolina but not like New York. Sometimes the buildings were so tall, that you couldn't even see the top of them from the ground without getting dizzy. Ivan was very familiar with the city. He knew all the places to go and things to see. I didn't have to think about anything for myself. Finally, I met a couple of girls around my age and they encouraged me to go to school and start doing things for myself. They said that depending on a man entirely was not a good idea. I started taking classes at Baruch. They had a pretty good accounting curriculum. At first I didn't tell Ivan about it because I wanted to surprise him after the first semester but he found out and became infuriated. That's when the beatings started."

"So you didn't attempt to leave him at that point?"

"No, I just figured he was upset because I went behind his back. I mean we had been married for five years and this was the first time he had struck me."

"Angelica, you didn't deserve that, there was absolutely nothing wrong with you trying to better yourself. I admire that. I'm just sorry he can't see what all of this has done to you and what it continues to do."

He placed his arms around her to comfort her then told her that things will work out just fine.

"Angel, do you trust me?"

"Yes, I trust you. I don't believe you mean me any harm."

"Good, then I want you to believe that I'm going to get you out of this mess and you will receive all those things you wanted when you married Ivan?"

"Well what things are you speaking of?"

"Well, for one thing, you said you wanted to travel. I will take you anywhere in the world you would like to go. How's that for starters?"

"Sounds great."

"But, I will first have to make certain you're better. Tomorrow I will be taking you to a facility where a colleague of mine works. He will have a room prepared for you under the name Regina Weston. Your husband will not be able to find you there since you will not be listed under your own name. After Dr. Bradley clears you to leave, I will take a couple of weeks off and we'll fly to Paris. How does that sound?"

The excitement within her was so great, she could barely sit still. After four torturous years with her husband, a complete stranger comes into her life to fulfill her lifelong desires.

"I don't know what to say. You don't know how happy that would make me."

"I want you to be happy. I want you to love me."

He couldn't believe what he had just said. He would have never said something like that outright. Of course, once something is said, there is nothing you can do but follow though with it.

"So, are you hungry?" I'll fix something real quick. Do you like waffles? I have a box of Belgian waffles in the freezer."

"In the freezer," she laughed. "What happened to home cooked meals?"

"Well what do you expect, I don't have a wife. Bachelors don't do a whole lot of cooking. But if it would make you happy, we can stop by the supermarket and pick up something."

"No, that's all right, waffles it is."

He led her into the kitchen where he toasted the waffles and poured maple syrup over them. After breakfast, she returned to the living room. She reclined on the couch in a comfortable position. The sight of her laying there with her robe dangling at her sides revealing her nude slender body excited him.

"Doc I feel sick!" she said with her lips puckered up in a seductive pout.

"What can I do to make you feel better?"

Using her index finger, she gestured for him to come to her. He shook his head no. Again, she called him, when he didn't come to her she sat up on the chair and began to chase him. He ran upstairs and into the bedroom. When she had finally caught up to him, he was laying on the bed with all his attributes exposed. Contrary to his name, he was a black man with caramel skin. His eyes were a deep and meaningful green. His hair was thick with large, wavy curls. Handsome was an understatement because his looks demanded attention.

His manhood stood up ready to perform when he heard her nearing the room. Angelica stood at the door watching him. Steve laid his silk robe across the foot of the bed allowing it to spill onto the floor like a red carpet welcoming her to come to him. Angelica knelt to her knees and crawled over to him like a hungry lion at its prey. She kissed his feet, legs and thighs right up to his pulsating staff. Although it was a first for her, it came natural. She positioned her lips around him allowing her mouth to slide down his shaft slowly then up again. When she hit a spot that caused him to react uncontrollably, she continued to please him. He covered his face with the pillow to keep from making any sudden outbursts. He turned her around and allowed her to sit on his face. They unselfishly pleased each other in more ways than one.

Their bodies joined to become one. Angelica held him tightly wishing that their togetherness would never end. Meanwhile, Steve gently caressed her, never breaking contact. He made a vow to himself that no one would come between them, not even her husband. As their passion juices flowed their connection to each other grew even stronger and somehow they knew the feeling was mutual.

CHAPTER

8

At the precinct, Richard waited in the interrogation room for the officer to return. He needed to come up with a solid alibi. "I could say that I worked late in the office. Sheryl could collaborate that because she had to work overtime herself. She didn't leave the office until seven o'clock. After that I went home and went to bed." He was concerned that somehow or another he would be the blame for what happened to Bob due to circumstantial evidence. Rich tapped on the table to drown out the unnerving silence of the room.

Officer Brown along with his edgy sidekick returned to the room.

"So Mr. Davis, did you have enough time to sort out an alibi?"

It was almost as though they read his mind.

"You know we always give our suspects time to think about what they will say just to show them that we're smarter than they are!"

He stood there with his hair slicked back from sweat. His shirt was ruffled as though he just got out of a fight. His partner, Officer Griswold stood there like a toy soldier with his hand on his weapon ready to shoot if he had the slightest movement.

"You see my partner here, he doesn't like men like you. He believes that the court system is a waste of time and that criminals such as yourself should be shot down without the privilege of denying your crime. That's what you were about to do wasn't it? Deny the crime?" He waited for an answer. "Well look, since this isn't the Wild West, I'm going to give you the benefit of the doubt but you'd better not waste my time or ol' Billy here will have to lay a hurtin' on your head. Do we understand each other?"

Rich watched him, his lips didn't make a move. He realized that he was not going to get a fair hearing, at least not in this precinct. If he made it to court in one piece, he would be lucky. He nodded his head in agreement because the last thing he wanted was for the officer to strike him to draw his attention when he heard him perfectly the first time.

"So Mr. Davis tell me, where were you the night prior to Barbara Givens death?"

"I'm not sure, what time are we talking about?"

"That was pretty smart. I see you're paying attention. Oh let's say ten o'clock."

"A.m. or p.m.?"

"P.m."

"I was at home in my bed."

"Is there anyone who can verify that?"

"No. I live alone."

"I see. Did you call anybody prior to getting into bed?"

"No. I just went to bed. I had worked long hours and was tired so I just went to bed."

"I see. Now I recall you saying something about you being intimately involved with the deceased. You don't mind if I call her that, do you? I mean she is deceased isn't she?"

He didn't wait for an answer because he knew that it was perfectly fine especially since he was the one carrying the magnum.

"You mean to tell me a foxy woman like that, you would prefer to go home and sleep. Man if it was me I'd be hurrying over to ride that, of course unless you're gay or something."

"Like I said before, I was tired and went home to get some sleep."

The officer looked back at his partner with a grin.

"Ya hear that Billy, he was too tired to see his girl-friend."

"She wasn't my girlfriend, she was my employer."

"She was more than your employer. People don't go around fucking their boss and their boss certainly wouldn't leave ten million plus her estate to an employ-ee. So please help me understand why she would do a thing like that."

"Because she has no family to leave it to and she wanted me to continue the business."

"What the hell would she care about the business continuing if she was dead? She has no children or siblings to leave it to. Her parents were killed some three years ago. The assailant got away. So now there's no one left but her right hand man to take over things. Isn't that right Richard?"

"You're twisting things." Richard insisted.

He leaned close to him so that Rich could look directly into his cold blue eyes.

"Tell me something Rich; did you kill her parents too, just to make certain that there was no one else around to become the beneficiary? Then encouraged her to make you the sole heir of her estate with a vow to keep things going?"

"No, she asked me to do that for her."

"Why would she do that? Now Rich remember I told you that we were going to be honest with each other?"

He leaned even closer to him so that his breath was hot against his face. He pulled his pistol from its hol-ster and placed it on the table in front of Rich. His partner stepped behind him waiting for Rich to make a move.

"Remember when I told you that telling the truth was important and I hope that you really thought this thing through. I gave you enough time to recount the events of last week so please answer this question correctly because it's giving me a migraine and your answer will either become Motrin or a beating drum. Are you ready for the question?"

Rich was shaking in his boots. He wondered if yelling would help. Would someone hear him and come to his aide?

"Now I'm going to ask you this one time. Listen to where I'm taking this before you answer. I don't want you to hang yourself. This is truth time here. Two months prior to Barbara's parents' death, the report indicated that she revised her trust. Which had named her parents as the sole beneficiary with you as the ultimate or contingent? Now that makes me believe that you would have enough reason to kill them. Do you see my problem with that?"

Rich just listened to him. He clearly understood what this was leading up to.

"Not only that," Officer Brown continued his theory, "the assailant waited another year to take her out of commission. She has a clean record without a debt to anyone. She paid all her bills in cash. Never on credit so she couldn't have owed anyone. Now here's where things point directly to you, she said in her will that if her death were to occur due to murder the first suspect should be you. Now why would she say that?"

Richard's face twisted with surprise. He knew that Bob had always been suspicious of him, but he thought she had long since gotten over that. This really complicated matters. This he couldn't explain.

"I don't know?"

Officer Griswold struck him behind the head with the butt of the gun.

"Billy didn't like your answer. He thinks you're lying. Would you like another opportunity to answer?"

"I have no idea why she would say something like that. I have done nothing less than work hard for that lady. I was her lover and friend. Bob had nobody. She was a cold woman and people didn't take to her too well. I was the closest thing to her. I loved her."

"Oh, so now you're telling me that you were more than just an employee. You see that Billy, he's starting to remember. Look what a good knock on the head will do for a guy. So tell us more about this relationship with Ms. Givens."

Rich hesitated a moment before speaking...

"Listen, it could have been anyone who killed her. She was a nymph. She screwed all of the guys who worked for her. She loved to intimidate them with their jobs and have them cheating on their wives. Besides, it could have been that new guy she just hired. She could have come on to him and made him angry. I don't know. All I do know is that I didn't kill her."

"Yeah that might very well be true but you're the only one gaining from all this."

"Look check him out. He probably got upset with her and beat her to death."

Billy looked at his partner and decided that perhaps he should pay the workers a visit.

"Alright Mr. Davis your petition is reasonable and we'll honor it but you had better not be sending us on a wild goose chase."

They escorted him to the door.

"You're free to go for now."

"You mean I didn't have to sit here?"

"Oh yeah, you had to sit here because we arrested

you. We're turning you loose for now until we gain some new evidence. We're going to check out those leads you just gave us."

Rich looked at the two guys wondering if they were setting him up like an attempted escape. He slowly walked through the door looking back with every step. When he reached the corner, he put some change into the phone and called the office and told Sheryl to send a car for him. He told her where he was and hung up the phone. He waited for Charles the driver to get there. Officer Brown and Officer Griswold stood at the precinct door watching him. They knew that he would foul-up and they would arrest him again except this time they would have concrete evidence.

When Charles pulled up in the company car, Rich got in and took a seat in back of the driver. He leaned back against the cushions relieved that the interrogation was over. He felt the spot on the back of his head where Officer Billy Griswold had struck him to see if the skin had been broken. When no blood was seen, he relaxed. He closed his eyes and recounted the events of that night. When he had arrived at Bob's house eight o'clock that morning she had been strangled and brutally raped. All she could tell him about the incident was that he had raped and choked her then left her for dead. That was his perfect opportunity to kill her and leave Ivan to go to jail for being stupid. If he was going to kill someone, the first thing he should have done is to make certain the victim was dead. He told her that he was going to call an ambulance but went downstairs in the garage and found a crowbar and began beating her in her chest, stomach and throat. After beating her, he told her thanks for the money she left him. He'd make certain to enjoy it. He returned the crowbar to the garage. He could see that she would be dying soon. He knew that she couldn't walk and certainly not use the phone because he mangled her hands and feet as well. He punched her in the face several times to make it look like someone hand wrestled with her first and beat her to death after raping her. He knew that Ivan had not raped her, she wanted it, he just didn't abide by her rules. Blood seeped out of her nose and mouth. He knew that she was hemorrhaging internally because he had damaged her organs. Death was eminent. Of course he didn't expect her to last till morning but that was okay because he would find her first with all the guys there to witness him finding her that way. He knew that Ivan would incriminate himself but he didn't, he remained cool and calculated.

When the guys had hurried upstairs, Ivan peered over his shoulder to see what was going on, then backed away. Bob tried to incriminate him so he knew that the only thing he could do was to suffocate her. He placed his finger over her nose and with his other hand covered her mouth to stop her from breathing. "Damn her," he thought. She was determined to live but destiny killed her. Now he had to build evidence against Ivan otherwise he was going to take the rap for his crime. Of course, if he hadn't tried to kill her first, he would never have taken the opportunity of finishing the job. "It was his fault. Oh yeah, Mr. handsome Carty, you will go down for this, there is no way I'm going to let you get away for killing my Bob."

Shortly after, Charles pulled in front of his home and Rich got out of the car. Thanks Charles. That will be all. He reached into his pocket and pulled out a fifty dollar bill and handed it to him through the driver's window. Charles thanked him for the tip and pulled out of the driveway to return to the driver's station.

CHAPTER
9

Ivan laid on his bed facing the ceiling wondering how something so simple could turn out to be so complicated. First he kills a woman, devises the perfect plan to cover his tracks, leave her for dead to find out that she wasn't dead at all, just unconscious. Now, his new boss is being questioned for the crime and all evidence is pointing to him because, life being the bitch that it is, he is the only one with a motive.

He thought about what the officer said..."Rich was fucking the boss." His scrawny, little body on top of Bob seemed ridiculous. He's probably small down there, he thought. He couldn't even imagine a little fellow like Rich riding on a tiger like Bob. Although she couldn't control a man like Ivan, she could definitely saddle his ride any day. Just thinking about her made him erect, the way she took him. Ivan looked down at himself, even for a hooker, he knew that it was a lot to take.

He remembered the first time he had made love to his wife. She was a virgin then, a young, pretty, country girl, looking for adventure. Her parents wanted her to grow up on the farm but he was able to sway her thinking. He told her that they were only moving a couple of towns away and that she would be able to see her folks whenever she wanted to. Of course, when opportunity permitted, Ivan would find jobs further and further away from her home making visits more and more difficult. Angelica was indeed a trained house girl. She knew how to keep things in order, have dinner prepared on time and learned the art of love-making pretty quick. She was everything he wanted in a woman. Finally, when he convinced her to go with him to New York, things changed. Within six months, they had moved three times and finally, he had her where he wanted her. She was the perfect young girl. She never wanted more than what was given and appreciated the simple things in life like movies, dancing, nothing special. She admired him and appreciated how hard he worked to take care of her until she met some new friends.

One thing Ivan knew about women, is that you never let them get together without you. Before he knew it, they had her sneaking around, going to school and doing God knows what. He couldn't bare the thought of it. When he got home that evening, she was in the kitchen preparing his meal as usual. It was never late. He asked her what she had done all day and she told him nothing. The insult angered him and caused him to reprimand her. That was just the beginning. She started telling the neighbors about him and trying to return home. He had to make certain that she remembered the vow she made to him..."till death do us part" and that would be the only way out. In thinking about her, her realized that he should be getting ready to go to the hospital to see her before visiting hours were over.

He took a quick shower and found something nice to put on. He figured she would appreciate his visit a little more if he walked into her room looking the way he did the first time they met. The monster that had abused her was now gone and they can start over again. He splashed Joop on his face and rubbed the balance over his sweater. He looked at himself in the mirror. He had dark eyes with thick, perfectly arched eyebrows, long, seductive lashes that always caught the attention of ladies. His broad shoulders and muscular arms was yet another asset which was an attention grabber. He was built like a Greek God. Muscles rippled across his stomach and chest. His arms were tight with bowling ball muscles. What more could a woman want? When he was pleased with his appearance, he put on his jacket and headed for the hospital.

He parked the car three blocks away because there was no parking space closer to the hospital. It had begun to rain heavily when he had only walked a block from the car. Of course that was typical in the fall. Ivan didn't find himself terribly concerned because it could have been worse, it could have been cold as well. The air was filled with the scent of rain and autumn leaves. The trees were yellow and burnt orange. The ground was carpeted by leaves and the earth was kissed by romantic scenery. Ivan wished he could bring his wife out to see all of this. Finally, he reached the information desk. He requested his wife's visitor's pass. While waiting for the pass, he noticed a man selling pretty bouquets of flowers. He purchased one for his wife. The arrangement was perfect. It had white lilies, lilacs, yellow tulips and other flowers he couldn't quite remember what they were. He returned to the desk and asked for the pass, when the attendant told him that there was no one in the hospital by that name. His response caught Ivan by surprise.

"I'm sorry, there must be a mistake. My wife has been in here for two weeks now. Certainly you must have mistaken. Could you take another look?"

"I'm sorry sir. I checked several times while you were purchasing the flowers. Maybe she was discharged. You can check with admissions."

Ivan's blood began to boil. He had taken just about enough of Dr. Painkin's crap. He hurried to the admissions area and waited for the secretary to notice him. When it was taking her too long, he called out to her.

"Excuse me." When she turned around to see who was speaking to her, she came over to the window.

"Hello sir, what can I do for you?"

"I'm looking for my wife, Angelica Carty. She was admitted into your hospital two weeks ago. I just stopped by last night to see her and she was still here. She was scheduled to remain here for at least four weeks according to her doctor. Now the attendant at the information desk is telling me that he doesn't have anyone here by that name."

"Maybe it's just an error; let me pull her chart to see where she is. Maybe they changed her room and it wasn't listed in the computer yet. What did you say that name was again?"

"Carty. Angelica Carty."

She disappeared through a door which Ivan presumed to be the file room. She returned with her chart.

"Now let's see," she said while opening the file. "According to the file, she signed discharge papers at her own request and left the hospital around ten o'clock last night."

"Last night? I left here around nine o'clock last night. Certainly if she was leaving the hospital she would have told me. Besides, she never arrived at home. So where is she?"

"I don't know sir, once a patient leaves the hospital against medical advise; it's up to them to get home. She didn't indicate anything else here."

"That's got to be an error; Angelica would never

leave like that."

"Is this your wife's signature?"

She held the chart to the window so that he could look at it. After scrutinizing it, he realized that it was indeed her signature.

"Thank you ma'am," he said then left the window. He started pacing the floor wondering if something had happened to her. He recalled how she looked last night when he saw her. She was still in her hospital clothes and gave no indication of leaving. Then he realized that it must have been a ploy by her doctor. She was still in the hospital, but in a different room. He would check the hospital room by room, patient by patient until he found his wife. He went to the floor she was supposed to be on. He started in the East wing, after checking each bed and not finding her, he went to the North wing. He checked each bed there, no Angelica. He started checking the West wing when he noticed the nurse that didn't like him. He stepped into one of the rooms and waited until he saw her pass then continued checking the other rooms. When he had gotten to the last room where his wife used to be, he saw that her bed was being occupied by someone else. That was the last room in that wing and there was only one more on that floor. He checked the corridor for the nurse, when he didn't see her, he quickly hurried down the hallway until he reached the turn off to the South wing. He knew that she was probably somewhere in this wing. It took him another 35 minutes before he realized that she was not there. He wondered if he should check the rest of the floor but decided that he probably would not find her there.

He went to the men's room and stared at the wall trying to decide what to do next. On his way out of the bathroom, he bumped into the nurse.

"Hi, Nurse Green, could you tell me where my wife is, they apparently changed her room last night and I can't seem to find her?"

"Mr. Carty!" She exclaimed. "Your wife signed herself out last night sometime after my shift changed. She didn't go home?"

"No, I wouldn't be here if she was at home."

"Well I don't know what to tell you but she isn't here."

"Do you know why she left in such a hurry? Or if someone picked her up?"

"Not as far as I know, let me check with Carol or Tammy, they were on duty last night after I left, they might know."

She escorted him to the nurse's station so that she could ask Carol if she knew anything about the patient that signed herself out late last night. Of course she knew what happened to the patient but it was the best way to deter his thinking.

"Carol, what happened to the patient that was in the room all the way at the end of the West wing?" She had to think a moment..."Who was the patient again?"

"Angelica Carty, the one that you told me left after I took her vitals last night."

"Oh yeah, the pretty one that was under Doctor Painkin's care due to acute hematoma. I know who you're talking about. Michelle is the one who gave her the papers last night. I only heard part of the conversation. She said something about having to get out of here. She looked pretty upset and shaky when she demanded the papers. Michelle told her that she would have to wait until her doctor returned but she refused and when Dr. Roberts stopped at the desk, she told him that she was leaving right now with or without the doctor's signature. He told her that she needed to sign a form that said she was leaving against medical advice and relieved the hospital of any repercussions that might follow as a result of her leaving. She nodded in agreement and he gave her the form, she signed it and left the hospital."

"Why didn't anyone contact me to let me know that she was leaving the hospital?"

"First of all, she is a grown woman and does not require permission to make decisions. She was not in prison here, she was a patient. Second of all, when we have patients come in here for domestic violence, we certainly wouldn't be the ones responsible for returning them to the hands of the assailant."

She directed her cold callus eyes directly at him making certain that he got her point.

"So, if you don't have any further questions, I have patients to see."

The nurse turned and walked away from him and started making her evening rounds.

Ivan became enraged. For some reason, this hospital seemed to have taken a personal interest in his wife and now his wife was missing and he had no clue how to come in contact with her. Anyone involved would be punished severely for making his life miserable. Angelica must not have gotten his point when he spoke to her last night. He would have to teach her a lesson when he caught up with her.

In the rain, he made his way back to his car. He unlocked the door and snatched it open. He got into the car closing the door behind him. He saw nothing but darkness as his temples throbbed from the tension of anger. He started beating the steering wheel trying to subdue his anger. He placed the key into the ignition and started driving aimlessly. He circled the neighborhood hoping to catch a glimpse of her but she was no where in sight. He decided that he would return home in case she decided to call. On the way home he decided to stop by the Seven Eleven store to pick up something to eat.

He went to the frozen food section and picked up a Salisbury steak entrée.

"Hello big guy. Missed me already huh?"

"Geneva isn't it?" He questioned confirming her name.

"Yeah, that's right. I was hoping to see you again. I think you acted pretty rude the last time. TV dinner huh, wife must be angry."

"Yeah, we're kind of on shaky ground right now. Hey listen, I'm sorry about the other day. I didn't mean to come off like that. It's just that you caught me off guard that's all. By the way, my name is Craig."

"Well listen, I was just about to punch out maybe we can share a drink together or something." Of course she was thinking more on the something side. She was just what he needed, somebody to get his frustrations off on.

"That sounds nice but I got to tell you, I'm no good at this kind of thing. I haven't socialized with other women since I got married."

"That's okay, whatever you don't know I'll teach you." She teased.

He looked at her out of the corner of his eye with a sexy grin. He had the deepest dimples which made his features more admirable. He was a clean cut man and even though he was soaked to the core, he still looked delectable. Geneva admired every bulge his wet clothes revealed.

"Listen, I'll wait for you outside in the car. Do you drive?"

"No, I was going to catch a bus up the street. I

don't live far from here. Maybe you would like to accompany me home so we can sit down and talk without the noise of the bar."

"Sounds great, I'll see you in a little bit." Ivan paid for his TV dinner and returned to his car. No one paid attention to his conversation with Geneva. The cashiers were busy handling customers. In fact, the other cashier didn't recognize him from her talking to him before. He returned to his vehicle and waited for her to come out. When she came out, Ivan got out of the car so that she would know where he was. She dashed through the rain in her tight powder blue jeans. She got into the car.

"This is a very nice car, what kind of work do you do?"

"Anything in the construction business but I only handle large jobs with companies that pay well."

"So you don't really have a steady employer?"

"No not really, I'm usually hired on a project by project basis by big contracting companies and I run the show until the job is done then I move on to other projects."

"No one's ever offered to keep you on the payroll?"

"Sure, but I'd rather work this way because it pays more money. I look at the various projects to determine which would be more profitable for me."

Ivan spewed out his lies as though he had rehearsed a script. He couldn't have her knowing how and where to reach him so he immediately shut that door before she asked for his number.

She directed him to her home which was only a mile away from the Seven Eleven supermarket. "So, do you live alone?"

"Yes, my mother thinks I should come back home but I like it on my own."

"How old are you?"

"Seventeen.	My birthday is in another three months."

"December. Are you a Sagittarius?"

"Yeah, how did you guess?"

"Your month and attitude goes together."

She escorted him to her apartment and unlocked the door. She was renting a basement apartment from an elderly lady. It was a nice, modestly furnished apartment, nothing like his but nice none-the-less. When he entered, she took his coat and told him to remove his shoes so that he wouldn't wet her carpet. She placed his shoes next to her own in the door way.

"Would you like me to put this into the dryer for you?"

"Sure thank you."

She went upstairs and found a robe that she thought would be big enough for him. When she returned, Ivan was scanning some pictures she had displayed on her wall unit. She had a number of pictures of herself, some alone and others with friends. There was one that beckoned him to pick it up. It was a picture of her with his weasel boss, Richard. What the hell was this young girl doing with Richard?

"Who is this dorky looking guy?" Ivan asked when he noticed her behind him.

"If you want, you can put this on and I will dry those wet clothes for you as well. They won't take long to dry." She took the picture from him and noticed it was the picture of her and Richard.

"He's just some old prick that I used to date. He still comes around from time to time, but I don't like him much."

"Why not? You two seem pretty close in this picture."

"Looks can be deceiving. He was a nice guy before, but he's a control freak. I hate those types. A couple of times he's smacked me around a bit, but nothing I couldn't handle. My girlfriend doesn't like him much. She told me to leave him alone before he accidentally kills me."

"Your friend seems like a pretty smart person. Why didn't you take her advice?"

"I tried, but he won't stop coming around. But anyway, he pays my rent and keeps money in my pocket. So what if I have to let him bury his head in me every now and again?"

Ivan shrugged. It sounded really sad hearing it from her side, but "women can be tricky," is what his father always told him. She probably met Richard the same way she met him, flirting at the Seven Eleven store.

He agreed to let her dry his clothes. She led him to the bathroom where he could remove his wet clothes and put on the robe. He handed them to her through the door and returned to the living room. She took his clothes, put them in the dryer and set the temperature to medium for sixty minutes. She joined him in the living room and turned on some soft music.

"So tell me, what made you move out of your parents' house?" he asked her when she was seated comfortably.

"I just needed to get away, build my own life, and do things on my own. Once you reach a certain age, you get the urge to do things that you know your parents wouldn't approve of so you move out. That way no one can say anything about what you do unless it's illegal or against your lease."

"I see, so is this what you moved away from your parents to do?"

"What do you mean?"

He leaned over and kissed her. She opened her mouth welcoming his tongue which gently caressed hers. She was soft and gentle just like Angelica. Although not a virgin, she was innocent to the experienced touch of a much older man. He placed his hand under her breast and fondled her nipple with his finger through her soft cotton shirt. She allowed him to gently force her back against the cushions on the chair. He towered her body with his own and pressed his covered body against hers.

She reached for his groin but he pulled her hands up over her head. Ivan placed his left hand between them so that he could open her tightly fitted jeans and then eased his hand down into her panties so that he could massage her tender flesh. She was so wet his fingers glided easily through it. He played with her pleasure pearl until he knew that her body was begging for his. Her saliva became overflowing as he teased her slowly pressing his index finger into her cave.

"Geneva," he whispered. "You want it?"

"Yes" she answered in the same tone.

"Then take it." He propped up on his knees to allow her to free him. When she had opened the robe and pulled his underwear down, her mouth wrapped around him and for the first time he felt something he had never experienced before. He had heard people talking about it and became turned off but to feel the intensity of the pleasure, it was beautiful. Her tongue danced circles around his tip while she worked her mouth back and forth over his shaft. He ached for her. Her mouth became juicier as she sucked him. He wondered what it was like for her to do that.

"Do you like doing that baby?" Ivan genuinely asked her.

"Yeah, you like it?"

"I love it."

"You've never done it before?"

"No."

"Let me show you how to reciprocate."

She laid down on the sofa so that he could try it. He knelt down between her legs and paused.

"It's the same as kissing. Here let me show you where." She pulled his face closer to her and placed his lips on her clitoris. He opened his mouth and cautiously allowed his tongue to encircle the flesh. He presumed he was doing it correctly because she started moaning and pulling his face tightly to her. He allowed his tongue to move down to her cave and forced it into her, wiggling it around.

"Oh God," she cried out and her juices shot out into his face. He rubbed it around her mound then climbed atop her and passionately made love to her. He surprised himself at how gentle he was being toward her. He had never done his wife that way. Sex was a routine thing and although he knew she was pleased, he realized that he had deprived her of something special.

Her body thrust forward to meet his every move. She massaged his back and shoulders while he strived to reach an orgasm. When the feeling intensified, he pulled away from her grabbing his organ. He got up and walked to the rear of her house to where he presumed her bedroom to be and returned with a condom. She rolled it down his shaft and pulled him on top of her. He hammered himself into her and an orchestra of gratification serenaded the room. He held her tightly considering whether or not he would take her life. She reciprocated and held him wondering if they would have the opportunity of doing it again. He reached up and placed his hands on the base of her chest and massaged there moving closer and closer to her throat. He allowed his hands to rest on her neck and he could feel the throb of her juggler vein pounding against his fingers. She was so alive. Ivan felt a strange desire to kill. Since strangling Bob, he has become preoccupied with this new vitality. It gave him a sense of regeneration and power.

She kissed him gingerly on the lips looking up and into his eyes. She almost thought she saw something rancor and evil in them but decided that it was probably his normal after sex look. Geneva had introduced him to something he would never have tried and pleased him greater than he had ever been before and now he had to get rid of her because he would find himself wanting her and that couldn't happen because he loved his wife. His temples started throbbing again and he wanted very much to get this over with. The image of she and Richard flashed to his mind, then Richard and Bob, fucking. Did Richard kill Bob?

"Craig is something wrong?"

CHAPTER

10

Early the next morning, Dr. Painkin drove Angelica to the medical facility where his dear friend, Dr. Joseph Bradley had practiced Neurosurgery with him at Sloan Kettering. Although Painkin knew that Joe possessed a greater talent for the field, Painkin would never admit it. Of course working side-by-side with Joe taught Painkin a great deal about precision and patience. Painkin remembered what his good friend told him…"the ability to heal is a gift from God and if he is not with you in the operating room, you are destined to failure." That phrase never had a meaning to him until he was challenged with a condition so sever that no human could repair, and even if he had the skilled hands of his doctor friend, there was no way Angelica's life could have been preserved without the act of the stranger in the operating room.

When they arrived, he escorted Angelica to his friend's office. Dr. Bradley was currently in surgery. The nurse told him that he should be out soon. The patient was being taken to recovery. Angelica looked at the many plaques and achievement awards Dr. Bradley had covering two walls. He had pictures of his family on a shelf just over his desk…two daughters and one son. His wife had long, dark hair which was pulled up into a bun at the top of her head with two oriental pins going through them like those the Japanese women wear. The daughters resembled their mother and the son was almost an exact replica of the father. He must be pretty proud of his family, Angelica thought while appraising the pictures.

Feeling a little nervous, Angelica fidgeted with her skirt.

"Don't worry; you'll be all right here. Dr. Bradley will take good care of you and nothing will happen to you here." Painkin assured her. He held her hand firmly to reassure her. When his friend walked into the room, he glanced at Angelica nodding his head.

"I see why you're anxious to help this pretty young thing. She's absolutely beautiful, like a delicate flower."

Angelica blushed at his comment. Steve looked at her with approval and shook his friend's hand.

"So, Ms. Weston, how are you feeling today?"

"Good, thank you doctor."

Her eyes met his and for the first time, he realized that her eyes were grey. She had only a small trace under her eye that revealed her horrible experience. When she realized what he was looking at, she reached up to touch it.

"I'm sorry such a beautiful girl like yourself would have to go through something a traumatic as that. No one deserves to be treated that way. Besides, it's almost gone, barely noticeable, I'm just trained to notice these things."

He gave her a reassuring smile while pulling an empty file from his desk. He began to question her to get a general profile on her. Then Dr. Painkin gave him the medical terms and conditions.

"Okay Ms. Weston, I guess it's time to get you over to the x-ray room so that I can get a current MRI. The results will show me exactly what I'm dealing with. I don't like to take any chances with my patients. Sometimes there are tiny tears in the brain that the x-ray can't pickup so I like to do my own intensive studies. You don't mind that do you?"

"No, do whatever you must."

"Good, let's go, shall we?" He escorted them down the corridor to the elevators. He pressed the button for the fifth floor. The elevator went up three floors then Dr. Bradley escorted them to the MRI room. Angelica looked at the machine. She certainly didn't expect to see something as huge as that. Painkin noticed her hesitation.

"Don't worry my dear. You won't have to go completely inside, just your head and shoulders. I'll be right here; the thirty-five minutes will be over before you know it."

"I know, but I'm claustrophobic!"

"Oh, I see. Steve turned to his friend.

"I know what you're thinking Steve but we need her completely alert for this test." Dr. Bradley was not about to jeopardize the tests by sedating the patient.

"Angel, I'm going to give you a headset so I will be able to talk to you. I want you to keep your eyes closed and just listen to me. As long as you don't open your eyes, you won't realize where you are. I also need you to remain perfectly still so that this test won't have to be repeated. Can you do that for me?"

"Yes, I guess so."

"Just listen to my voice." He put his arms around her pulling her close to him. He kissed her on the cheek and whispered into her ear..."I'll talk to you about the other night."

She smiled and Dr. Bradley knew that his friend must have said something dirty to her because she had a bashful smile on her face and his cheeks extended from one side of his face to the other.

"Okay Angelica, this is it." Dr. Bradley told her. "The test will take approximately thirty-five minutes. What the MRI does is take pictures of the target area layer by layer. If there are any unnatural changes, adhesions, tears, lumps, bleeding or seeping, it will show up and any special attention or treatment will be administered. Of course, I don't anticipate any problems because you had an excellent doctor and surgeon working with you and he has never been wrong before in all the time I've worked with him. He takes his work very personal."

He told her to lay down on the table. He placed the headset over her head and a pair of goggles over her eyes to protect them from the electromagnetic rays.

"Ready?"

"Ready as I'll ever be," she said with apprehension to Dr. Bradley's question.

He slid the table into the machine and lined her up according to where he needed her. Angelica heard Dr. Bradley speaking to her in the headset.

"Okay Ms. Weston, I'm starting the test. I need you to be perfectly still. Any movements can cause the test to come out falsely or unclear and it will have to be repeated."

"I'm here darling," Steve reassured her. He started singing softly in her ear a song by Howard Hewett "Show Me."

She imagined herself floating on the Caribbean Sea; she could just feel the heat. Before she knew it, she was being pulled out from the machine and her eyes were being uncovered.

"Hello Angel. You see that didn't take long did it?"

As her eyes slowly adjusted to the light, he became clearer to her. His voice was soft and gentle, soothing to her terrified soul.

"I'll have the results in about twenty minutes. You two can go and catch lunch in our cafeteria and then return to my office and I'll let you know what we're dealing with." Dr. Bradley told them as he left the room.

Steve and Angelica went downstairs to the cafeteria and picked up something to eat. They found a table next to the window looking out at a beautiful flower garden with a waterfall just across the yard. His heart raced while looking at her. He cupped her hands in his.

"This might seem preposterous or even crazy to you but I'm falling in love with you. It seems as though we have been together for a long time and I don't want to let you go."

"That sounds beautiful Steve. You are a very special man but things are moving just a little too fast for me. I do have a growing feeling for you but I can't say that it's love yet although I can see myself falling in love with you."

Steve was about to say something when they were interrupted by someone Angelica knew.

"Angelica, how are you?"

Angelica looked up at the woman speaking to her. Surprised, it was her co-worker Sandy.

"Hello Sandy, what a pleasant surprise. What brings you to this neck of the woods?"

"My mom is a patient of this hospital, she's upstairs on the fourth floor. I needed to get something in my stomach before I pass out. You know how it is when you've been sitting in the hospital all day without eating. Enough talk about my problems. Why haven't you been to work?"

Steve listened closely, awaiting Angelica's response. He wondered whether or not she would reveal the cause of her condition.

"I was in a terrible accident and had to remain in the hospital for some time to heal."

"Are you all better now?" Sandy asked trying not to pry any further. She knew that if there was something Angelica wanted her to know in detail she would have already mentioned it.

"Well, not quite, I will have to remain in care of my doctor until I have fully recovered."

"Is this your doctor?"

"No. He's a friend of mine."

Steve was fascinated at how fast Angelica could give answers to questions she was uncomfortable answering. More than that, how she was able to maintain a straight face while saying it.

"I stopped by your house about a week ago. Your husband told me that your mother was sick and you were out of town seeing about her. How is she?"

Angelica felt heavy throbbing. Sandy had caught her by surprise with a question she did not know how to answer. She had gained a great deal of experience telling half truths about situations since she had been covering up for her husband's abuse for so long. Now her co-worker threw a monkey wrench in her works and she hadn't a clue how to respond to it.

"She's doing much better thanks. Listen, I would love to continue chatting with you but I have to hurry up and have lunch so I can get back for my results. Catch up with you later."

Sandy understood the cue and said goodbye. She wondered who that handsome fellow was sitting with Angelica. As long as she had known Angelica, she never knew her to cheat on her husband so her best summation was that he was a good friend or a relative. Besides, she had a damn good looking man at home. Any woman would be at his beck and call.

"Do you always cover up for your husband's actions?" Painkin asked genuinely.

Taken aback, her expression changed. Why would he ask her such a question when he knew how sensitive she was about the situation? Angelica allowed her eyes to drop to her plate and he caught her chin.

"I'm sorry, I didn't mean to offend you, it's just that I didn't expect you to lie to your co-worker like that. You mean to tell me that they don't know about it?"

"Look at my husband. Who would believe that he would harm anyone? He appears to be kind and gentle. He has very loveable ways and most women find him highly attractive and wouldn't look past his debonair stature, so don't go pointing your finger at me for trying to keep from exploiting myself."

"You're right. I shouldn't have said that, I take it back. Are we friends again?" He cast his puppy eyes on her pleading for forgiveness."

"Okay. I'll forgive you this time but the next time I'll have to spank you!"

"You promise." His answer struck her funny and a burst of laughter filled the once solemn room. "We should be getting back, I'm sure that Dr. Bradley should have your results now."

He got up from the table and walked around to where she was sitting so that he could help her from her chair. "Thank you."

"Anything for you, madam."

They returned to Dr. Bradley's office and waited for him to finish his rounds. His nurse paged him to let him know that they were in his office. Shortly after, Dr. Bradley walked into the room. He looked at Angelica strangely then at Dr. Painkin as though he was waiting for the punch line to a joke.

"Is there something wrong Dr. Bradley? You look like you've seen a ghost or something." Angelica asked.

Dr. Bradley scanned the contents of the file and

began explaining the findings.

"The injuries described in your notes indicated that she suffered severe trauma to the right side of the brain. It also indicates that there was a removal of a large sized Hematoma which would have left some form of mastation that would have shown it was there even if her recovery time was faster than usual."

"So, what's the problem? I don't understand." Painkin said with a curious look on his face.

Dr. Bradley didn't say another word. He only handed the report over to Dr. Painkin and allowed him to look at the results of the MRI scan taken earlier. Steve took the file and quickly read over the results of the test. Angelica watched him waiting for a reaction. He returned his eyes to the top of the page and slower than the first time scanned the content of the report. He turned the page and continued to read. He started smiling and quickly closed the file.

"So...." Dr. Bradley questioned..."What is your conjecture?"

"A miracle has occurred here. Not only has all evidence of the incident been erased, she is in perfect condition. No further treatment is required, she can go home!"

"I don't understand. You called me up, demanded my expertise, and made me bend my rules to tell me that there is absolutely nothing wrong with this patient!"

Steve walked over to his friend and told him that he appreciated all of his help and he would take care of things from this point on.

"Don't you even attempt to walk out of here without giving an explanation for this fiasco. I want to know what is going on here," he demanded!

"I'm sorry buddy. I don't have an answer for you.

I'm just glad that things turned out the way they did. Now, I'll call you at a later date and we can chat about it but as for right now, I've got some celebrating to do."

CHAPTER

11

Officer Brown summoned eight of his best officers and gave them instructions.

"You two," he pointed to two of his officers..." I want a tap placed on every phone line in Mr. Davis' office. If there is one in the bathroom, I want it tapped too. I want to know what he's saying at all times. I want every conversation recorded. I'm sure this guy will give us a cue; he won't be able to keep this thing inside him for long. I want you two to take care of his house. The first opportunity you get inside I want you in there. The rest of you, I want the Givens' property to be examined from top to bottom until something can be found that will point a finger at somebody. I, along with Officer Griswold, will question the employees and neighbors of Ms. Barbara Givens. Have I made myself clear?"

Everyone nodded their heads.

"Good, I want to hurry up and close this one guys." The officers left the station and headed in the direction of their duties.

Officer Brown and Griswold went to the Givens Corporation and found the receptionist, Theresa at the desk.

"Hi, I'm Officer Brown and this is my partner Officer Griswold, we're here investigating the murder of Barbara Givens and I need to ask you a few questions. Would now be a good time?"

"Not really" she exclaimed. "Perhaps we can talk when I take my lunch at about 1:30."

Officer Brown looked at his partner and told her that he would meet with her at 1:30 over lunch. She smiled at him when the phone rang.

"Waterman Givens Contracting, may I help you?" she said in the receiver as she answered the phone. The officers stood there waiting to see who was calling. When the person on the other line began to speak, she turned her back to the officers and started whispering into the receiver...

"Rich, this isn't a good time, there are two police officers here questioning me about the death of Barbara Givens."

"What did they ask you?"

"Nothing, I told them that now wasn't a good time to talk, that I had a lot of work to do."

"Did they ask you anything about me or mention my name or my relationship with Bob?"

"No. Why what's going on?"

"Nothing. I just wanted to know what kind of questions they were asking. I need you to remain at the office late today. Try and stall them until tomorrow."

"I can't she said in a low tone. I already told them that I would be available to speak with them at 1:30!" She said in an even lower tone with a mark of exasperation in her voice.

"Listen to me Theresa. If you want to keep that hefty check you're getting, you'll do exactly what I tell you. They're trying to pin this thing on me. I already told them that I would never do anything to hurt Bob but they wouldn't believe me. So I need to make certain that you don't bring up something that might give them the impression that I had something to do with her death. Can you understand that?"

"Yeah, so what do I tell them?"

"Don't worry about that, I'll call you with work later at 1:25 which will make you unable to answer any questions. I'll talk to you later. Start pulling files so that they won't think anything of this call."

"Don't you worry about a thing Mr. Connor; as soon as Rich comes in I will have him call you about that contract. I don't know sir; I have no authority to send men out on a site. You will have to wait until I speak with Rich; he's the one who handles that. Let me have your number and I'll make certain that Rich knows that this call is urgent."

She wrote a number down on the piece of paper and put it into Rich's box then hung up the phone. She walked into the room behind her and started pulling files. She returned with a stack of files in her hands and began making phone calls. The officers watched her for a moment then while walking away, told her that they would see her at 1:30.

"What did you make of that call?" Griswold asked his partner. "I can't really be sure but I would suspect that it was her boss because she became very secretive for a while there."

"Do you think our boys got a tap on it?"

"I don't know but I hope so. I got a feeling this thing is going to be easier than we expected. However, I think we should check back with her at 1:30. Her response will tell us whether or not it was her boss. If it was Rich on the phone, then he will try to occupy her time so that she won't be able to give us any information."

"What now?"

"Let's get over to the Givens place and have a little chat with the guys. We need to get a little personal history on her background. I'm sure that someone knows something."

In the meantime, Rich dialed Ivan Carty's number. He would frame him for Bob's murder and let him take the rap for what happened. Besides, he had already attempted to kill her he just didn't finish the job. The one thing Ivan didn't know about Bob was that she would never die quietly. In a matter of speaking, Rich felt that he saved Ivan's ass. If Bob had been able to talk to the police prior to their little run in, he wouldn't be in this predicament right now trying to cover his tracks. He listened a while longer waiting for someone to answer but the phone only rung. "Where the hell is he? Not even his alleged wife seems to be home. What kind of relationship does these two have?" Then it came to him, he would have the officer's check out his relationship with his spouse, perhaps he's an abuser or something and that will point a finger at him to show that he has another side. The problem would be proving that he dealt with her.

Officer Griswold received a call by radio..."Where are you guys now?"

"We're at the Given's Corporation. Why what's up?"

"I think you two should check out Twin Pine Drive, there had been a murder not too far from the Barbara Given's place."

"Who's on it?"

"Tom and Larry are there right now but they are expecting you."

"I'll be there in about twenty minutes." Billy told Officer Brown what was going on and they hurried over to Twin Pine Drive. As they had expected, a series of squad cars were in the driveway marking the spot. They entered the house through the basement. The owner was outside talking with Larry and Tom. Officer's Brown and Griswold found forensics taking shots of the body.

"How old would you say she is?"

"No more than eighteen."

"Must have been someone she knew, there was no forced entry and no signs of rape. Just a clean, easy break." He looked at the pathologist.

"No struggle at all?"

"None what so ever. Her neck was snapped in one easy motion. Here, take a look at her face, see how relaxed the muscles are? Probably after she reached her orgasm he talked with her for awhile and when he saw that she was comfortable he placed his hands on the sides of her face and twisted her neck."

"Someone would have to be good to do something like that without her realizing that something was wrong!"

"No. Just strong!"

While Griswold continued to speak with forensics, Officer Brown searched the house for any photos, address books, notes, etc. He called out to his partner..."Hey Billy, guess what I found?"

"What is it?"

"It's a photo of Mr. Davis and the young girl. They seem pretty intimate too. Couch scene at that."

"You mean Richard Davis?" Griswold asked surprised.

"Yeah, and he's got his hands around her neck too. This guy seems to have a thing for choking women. Barbara Givens was strangled as well."

"I guess she just wouldn't die so he had to beat her to death. Let's talk to the neighbors to see if any one knows about their relationship. Then we'll pick him up for questioning."

"He's going down this time. There's no escaping."

Griswold told forensics to bag up the photos. There was a woman at the door trying to get in but Tom prevented her from entering the house.

"Tom, let her in, perhaps she will be able to shed some light on this." Griswold said to the officer at the door.

Tom stepped out of the way and let the cute Spanish girl through. Her hair was pinned up in a thick, twisted ball at the crown of her head with curls hanging down from the ball to the back of her neck. She had pretty hazel eyes which were narrow at the corners. Her lips were shaped like a heart and her cheeks were big and round like apples.

"Hi, my name's Maria Santiago, my friend Geneva lives here. What happened?" Her Spanish accent was very strong.

"Your friend Geneva was murdered last night. Perhaps you might know who did this."

Maria backed away with her hands over her mouth..."I told her to leave that guy alone. I told her that he was too old for her but she wouldn't listen. He didn't love her; all he wanted was control. One time he came over to the store and pulled her between the isles and started slapping her because some guy had spoke to her. Can you believe that shit? Right then I knew that he would really hurt her some day, and now she's gone."

"Do you know what that guy's name is?" Officer Griswold asked.

"I think his name was Richie. He was some ritzy guy with money. He has temper tantrums when things don't go his way."

Officer Brown called over forensics..."Let me have that photo a minute."

The photo was handed to him.

"Is this the guy?" He asked, holding up the photo so that she could get a good look at it.

"Yeah, that's the bastard. As you can see, he had a thing for dominating women. They were joking in that picture, but he's choked her before."

"Thanks. That's all I need."

"Can I see her?"

"You might not want to see her."

"Did he abuse her before killing her?"

"No. I don't think she even had time to realize that he was killing her or that he was going to kill her. In fact, I don't think he knew he was going to kill her until he did it."

She walked over to the body and Officer Brown motioned to his partner to lift up the cover. Maria looked at her dead friend. The cool she once displayed had diminished to tears. Seeing the many deaths over the years hadn't prepared her to see the cold stare of her best friend. It just wasn't the same as looking at a family member in a casket. In anger, she turned to Officer Griswold.

"He's not going to walk is he?"

"No, we're going to put Mr. Davis away for a very long time and with your help, we can do it much faster."

"Anything you need, just call me," she said while taking one last look at her friend. The officers escorted her outside while asking a few last questions. Maria willingly gave them the information they required which pointed out the fact that Richard was guilty of this hideous crime. She felt consolation in knowing that he would not get away. She imagined that he had done this before. Preying on young girls and beating them to death.

"Damn him to hell," she exclaimed while continuing to her car.

৵৵৵

Richard looked at his watch and realized that he had better give a call to the office before the officer's have the opportunity to question Theresa. She knew of the intimate relationship he had with Bob and knew that they had screaming matches every so often and he needed to make certain that she didn't bring any of that up.

"Hi Theresa, where are the officers now?" Richard asked when she answered the phone.

"I don't know, they received a call and hurried out earlier after I spoke to you. I haven't seen them since then."

"Did it have anything to do with me?"

"I don't know, they just answered a call."

Rich thought about it for a moment. He needed to get over to Bob's place before they find something they shouldn't.

Rich got into his car and drove over to Bob's house. The guys were out back working on the pool.

"Ivan, can I see you a moment?" Ivan looked up to see Rich standing at the sliding glass doors. He called David over.

"I have to speak to Rich for a moment; you take over for me until I get back."

Ivan was skeptical about Rich calling him from his work. In fact, last he knew, Rich was locked up for the murder of Barbara Givens. "What's up?"

"Ivan listen, we never really went over your profile or background so I would like to ask you a couple of questions."

"What brought this on? I've been working for this company for an entire month now and the work, I might add, is exquisitely done. So why are you questioning my background now? The only thing you should be interested in is whether I'm qualified for the job which I'm sure I've displayed already so let's stop the bullshit!"

"Good, I'm glad you've said that because I need to get right to the point since time is of the essence."

Ivan waited for him to continue. He could feel the muscles in his jaws tightening.

"Did Bob come on to you at anytime during or after work or perhaps do something that made you feel uncomfortable?"

"No, why do you ask?"

"She didn't make any sexual advances toward you?"

"What part about no didn't you understand? My relationship with Bob was entirely professional."

Rich had a shrewd grin on his face. He couldn't believe that Ivan wouldn't come clean and admit that she wanted to fuck him.

"Ivan, you mean to tell me that you don't remember fucking her?"

His bold statement took him by surprise and the question angered him.

"Excuse me!" He blurted out with his fist pressed at his side trying to keep himself from knocking this man through the wall.

"I know that you fucked Bob. I saw the whole thing. She asked you to stay behind and you fucked her."

Ivan didn't respond. His cool demeanor irritated Rich. He would get him to admit, at the very least, that he had an encounter with her.

"I'll take that your silence means that I've struck a positive note."

"No actually, you're wrong. I've never slept with Bob and if I did I wouldn't be sitting here talking to you about it. What goes on between a man and a woman in the privacy of their home should not be discussed, especially their sexual activities. So if you don't mind, I've got work to do."

"You killed her you bastard and left me to take the blame for it!"

"According to the police, you killed her and now you're trying to pin the blame on me. Besides, my wife is much prettier and I'd rather spend my time with her but thanks for the story anyway. It almost sounded real. "

Ivan started to walk away then turned to face Rich again.

"By the way, why did this Ivan guy kill his boss? Was the pussy that bad?" He laughed and walked away before Rich could answer him. There was no way he would get incriminating information from him. "It's bad enough the jackass doesn't have sense enough to know the house must be wired, but to try and get me to tell on myself, he must be crazy!" Ivan returned to work and David questioned him about his talk with Rich after noticing his change in persona.

"Hey man what's up? What did Rich want?"

"It's nothing man, he's under a lot of pressure these days and wanted to see if I could do something to help him out."

"What did he want you to do? Take the blame for him?"

Ivan just smiled. They continued working until four thirty in the afternoon. Rich remained in the house wondering how he was going to get Ivan to admit that he attempted to murder Bob. If he was going down, so would Ivan.

"Um, Ivan could you come here a moment?"

"Sure Rich, more stories to tell me?"

"Yeah, I want to tell you the one about the man who returned with you and raped Bob."

"You're hysterical. Desperation must be kicking in. But tell me anyway, I need a laugh after today."

"I'm going to the police with the information. I was trying to protect you before but now I've got to turn you in."

"Okay Rich." He shrugged walking toward the door. "Make certain that our checks are ready tomorrow. I don't want any bullshit when it comes to my pay and I'm sure the guys feel the same way."

He looked in the direction of the other four and waited for a response.

"That's right!" Jimmy said followed by Robert and Paul. "We want our checks on time, bills got to be paid."

Ivan and the guys got in their cars and left. Richard casually looked around the house. Ivan's response made him realize something he hadn't considered...the house must be tapped. Why else would they let him out...to get more information? What better way to convict a person than to wait until he shit on himself? He calculated what he had said to Ivan hoping that he didn't say anything that would directly incriminate himself. "Shit, I've got to be much smarter than this. I'm about to send myself straight up the creek. Damn, I'll be more careful." He turned off the lights and left Bob's house.

೭ა

Outside, Officers Thompson and his partner waited in unmarked cars a block away. They watched everything that went on in the Givens' house.

"What do you think of this Ivan character?" Officer

Thompson asked his partner.

"I'm not sure. I don't know what to make of him yet. He certainly doesn't seem concerned at the least about anything."

"That's exactly what makes him even more suspicious, the fact that he's so nonchalant about the situation. Look, I'll tell you what I've gathered about his personality. He probably didn't kill the woman but may have contributed to the situation or at the very least know something about it."

"Even if he fucked her, I don't think he killed her. Listen to this Rich character; he's practically admitting that he killed her. What I think is that this Ivan character might have attempted to hurt her and fell short of the job and this Richard guy finished the job. Only problem is the ball fell in his lap and not Ivan's. So he's hoping that Ivan will say something that will point things back in his direction and take the heat off himself."

"I think you might have a point there. But for argument sake, let's keep an eye on this Ivan character until this thing is settled."

"Okay, so are we going to keep a trace on this Rich character?"

"Let's see where he's going."

"No, I've got a feeling that he'll be back. He probably realizes that we're watching him so he'll come back sometime later tonight when he thinks it's safe. There must be something he wants to remove from the house."

"Good idea." Officer Thompson sat back in the seat watching Richard drive off. He knew that it was going to be a long night.

CHAPTER

12

Ivan pulled off his clothes and jumped into the shower. He couldn't stand another moment of debris against his skin. He lathered his body with Irish Spring, he loved that scent, it always gave him the feeling of "real" clean. After allowing the water to knead into his tired muscles, he changed into something a little more comfortable.

In the living room, he reclined in his easy chair allowing the lasting aroma of his shower soothe him. He realized that due to the situation at hand, he had to remain calm until this Bob thing blew over. It wouldn't be long before Rich would be sentenced for his crimes against his employer and his young girlfriend. Remembering that young slender body, Ivan felt himself rising. "She really was a piece of work that Geneva," he crooned. He could still feel himself atop her with his hands cupped around her breast and his organ embedded deep inside her. But of course, he needed her for greater things than sexual gratification. She would never know how much she helped him and there was no way he would have tainted her last moment by telling her that she was dying to frame her boyfriend. Ivan sat there content with himself knowing that he rewarded her prior to her sacrifice, because he knew that there was no way a square like Rich could handle young pussy like that, so he actually did her two favors - he saved her from ever having to pretend again and he gave her the best fuck of her life before she died. It was too bad she had no way of helping him find his Angelica. She would pay for causing him this much grief.

After a while, Ivan grabbed his jacket and headed for the door. Outside in the car, Ivan drove to the hospital where his wife was located. He went into the lounge and ordered something to eat. After paying for his meal he took hold of a seat at a table located at the rear of the diner. A young nurse was seated there having her dinner he presumed.

"Do you mind if I join you?" he asked.

She looked up from her plate to meet the eyes of the most handsome guy she had ever seen.

"Please, by all means, have a seat."

Ivan took a seat across from her and looked at his food.

"I guess the employee food is just as bad as the patients' huh?"

His statement caught her by surprise. She laughed and directed his attention to her own. "You should try a sandwich next time; you can never go wrong with pastrami and cheese with lettuce and tomatoes."

"Thanks, I wish I had known that about five minutes ago. So what's your name?"

"I'm Tammy, Tammy Jacobsen," she said smiling.

Ivan watched this woman blush at his every comment.

"My name's Sean, Sean Ray Travis."

"Where'd you get that name?"

"My folks gave me that name because it contains both my real father and my proposed father's names."

"Are you serious?"

"No, I just knew it would catch your attention. So are you from around here? I haven't seen you around before."

"Well, I'm kind of new here. I've only been on staff for three months."

"Do you like it here?"

"It's all right. They have too much politics going on for me, so I do my work and go home when shift change come up, unless I have to pull double shifts. So which department do you work in?"

"I don't work here; my cousin was in this hospital for a while and mysteriously discharged herself. No one has heard from her since about two weeks ago. I was trying to get some answers as to what happened. So far no one knows anything other than the fact that she did indeed discharge herself. It's not like her to disappear like that, without letting someone know where she is."

Ivan continued to feed her false information hoping that he would stir up enough feelings in her to recollect something that she might have heard.

"I'm sorry, as I said before, I'm new around here and I haven't heard anything going on like that. There have been no complaints mentioned about a patient being unhappy and leaving or anything. I wish that I could help!" She smiled weakly and continued to eat her sandwich. That was a really bizarre story, she thought. Why would someone just disappear like that? She sympathized with him but she hadn't heard anything otherwise she would try and help him. He had already been to the patient's file room and spoke to some of the nurses already. If they didn't give him any answers, probably it was top secret or they genuinely didn't know other than what actually happened.

Ivan changed the subject..."What do you like doing after work?"

"I enjoy bowling, rollerblading, working-out at the

gym, and other things like that. How about yourself?
What do you like doing?"

"Anything that makes women happy."

A woman looking at her wrist watch caught her
attention. "Oh, my break's over, I'd better be getting
back upstairs." In a flash, she had cleaned up her din-
ing space and dumped her tray. "It was nice chatting
with you Sean. Sorry about the rush."

Ivan ran and caught up with her. "Hey, how about
we get together sometime?"

Continuing to rush, she thought to herself, this guy
seems too mysterious to me. I'd better stay clear of him
although he is very attractive..."Nah, I don't think so.
The last thing I need is gossip going on about me
around here."

"We can meet away from the hospital. Besides, I
don't come here often.

"Well listen, I'm in a hurry but maybe we'll see each
other again. How about I pick you up tonight when
you get off?"

"Oh, I have a car. But thanks anyway."

"So..."

Before he could get his statement out, she stepped
into the elevator and pressed her floor. Ivan turned
and headed for the door.

"Damn, this is going to be harder than I thought."
He didn't get the response he was expecting or hoping
for. While on his way out, a doctor brushed up against
him while passing. Ivan turned around to see Dr.
Painkin.

"Excuse me, aren't you my wife's doctor?"

"Pardon me."

"Angelica Carty, you were her doctor!" he said again
attempting to help the forgetful doctor regain his memory.

"I'm sorry fellow, that may very well be true but I see a great deal of patients in a day so to remember even one by name would be impossible. Sorry."

He started to walk off when Ivan grabbed his arm. The doctor turned in his direction with a note of irritation in his eyes this time.

"Listen, I have not seen my wife in two weeks and I was told that she discharged herself which seems preposterous. So either your institution is hiding her or someone knows something about it."

"Mister, if you do not let go of my arm, I will have you thrown out of this hospital, on your ear before you could blink your eyes twice."

Ivan realized that he was still holding the doctor's arm. He apologized and motioned to compose himself.

"Dr. Painkin right?" he questioned to confirm that he had the name correct. "I don't want any trouble, I know that you recognize me and I know that you have animosity toward me because of my wife's situation but right now she's missing and I have no idea where to find her."

"Then maybe she doesn't want to be found. Have you ever considered that?"

"Angelica would never leave me."

"Maybe not, but right now she seems to be in hiding from you so perhaps she's changed her mind. Listen, I would love to continue this conversation but I have patients to see." He gave Ivan a quick threatening glare and walked away hoping that he got the message this time.

The doctor's arrogance angered Ivan, but he knew that there was nothing he could do about it. There was no physical evidence that would indicate that he had anything to do with Angelica's leaving other than him recommending it and he was under no obligation to reveal what he said to her. Ivan left the hospital and returned to his car. About three hours later he saw his new friend, Tammy leaving the building. He hurried over to her.

"Hey, I figured you would be getting off soon. I was just leaving when I noticed you coming out. You have any plans tonight?"

"No. I'm just going home to get some rest. Are you always this persistent?"

"Not unless I meet a woman who's as pretty as you are!"

She smiled...

"Alright, I won't make this difficult for you, how about we go some place neutral."

"Lead the way." Ivan walked her to her car and waited for her to get in and lock her door. Then he returned to his own car. She drove for about fifteen minutes and pulled into the parking lot of Houlihan's."

Ivan drove up next to her and turned off his engine. He hurried over to her door and helped her out. With the long trench she was wearing, he hadn't noticed the short, royal blue, velvet mini skirt she changed into since he sat down with her at the hospital.

"That skirt is really hot. You sure you want to go in there like that?"

"Don't be silly, let's go." She escorted him into the bar. Everyone greeted her as though this was her usual hang out spot. From the moment she entered the place a fleet of hugs and kissed showered her. Ivan presumed that the woman who showed them to a table was a good friend because she was whispering something to her as they neared their table.

"So, what's your friend's name?" Tanya asked while handing them a menu.

"Oh I'm sorry Tanya, this is Sean."

"Hello Sean, she greeted him while giving him a wink. "You must be pretty special for Tammy to bring you around her friends. It's been a long time since we've met any of her guy friends."

He turned and looked at her…"Is that right?"

The waitress smiled at the two of them and asked them what they wanted. Tammy ordered a martini and Ivan requested the same. She hurried over to the bar and ordered their drinks. She returned momentarily with the drinks.

"Ok guys, enjoy. Let me know if I can get you anything else." She walked away to give them privacy and noticed that another of her customers had an empty glass and that was a no no. All glasses must remain full. Full glasses meant more money.

"So Sean, tell me how is it a nice looking guy like you would be caught single?"

"I never told you I was single."

A look of confusion came over her face.

"Well you gave me the impression that you were unattached."

Ivan could see that he was losing good faith with her so he needed to clean up that statement quickly.

"What I meant was, my wife and I separated, not legally but she left me some time ago for another man. I haven't been able to deal with another relationship since then."

"That's too bad. Well listen, what you need is someone to occupy some of that time so that you won't have to think about it so much."

"I've got to tell you that I'm a little rusty at this companion thing. I may slip up and say or do the wrong thing."

"Don't worry, it will come back to you, once you've done it, it never leaves you." There was a commotion going on behind them. Ivan turned to see what was going on. Tammy watched his handsome features allowing her eyes to trace his muscular body. His size was formidable yet it was propitiating at the same time. While watching him, she wondered whether he was serious about not being involved with a woman in a long time or was this just another sorry pick up line.

Ivan felt her stare and turned to look at her. "Tammy what's wrong?"

"Nothing, I'm fine Sean."

"Are you sure? I felt you looking at me. Are you sure that there isn't any thing on your mind?"

"No, really, I'm fine. Hey, how about we go back to my place and talk a little while without the noisy crowd?"

"No. Not tonight. I have things I want to do. How about we do it tomorrow?"

"That will be fine. Tomorrow it is."

They left the bar and he escorted her to her car.

"Listen, I didn't offend you did I? I really didn't mean any harm. I just thought that we could spend some time alone together."

Ivan had a confused look on his face. Was she serious? Already she was willing to take him home not knowing whether or not her life could be in danger. They had only met hours ago and already, she wanted to take him to bed. He despised women like that. He would indeed oblige her when the time was right. Perhaps he would put his hands around that tiny little neck of hers and squeeze. Or maybe he would torment her first then find some sophisticated way of taking her useless life away. But of course, he knew that he couldn't. She would be the key to finding his Angelica. Someone in that hospital knew her whereabouts and he needed someone to find her for him. This woman would be the one. She was young, naive and already infatuated with him. He knew that it was only a matter of time before he could have her subconsciously snooping for him.

A flash of anger came over him as he thought about how his wife up and left the way she did. He told her that she would never get away from him. He would make certain that someone would pay for ruining his life. Angelica belonged to him and somehow, he knew that the doctor had something to do with it. He either had her transferred to another hospital or helped her get an apartment somewhere. Tammy would be the one to reveal her location.

"You know what, I've changed my mind. I decided that perhaps I will take you up on your offer. How about I go to your place tonight?"

For a moment, she thought that she had lost her touch with men and became one of the unattractive people.

"Sean listen, you don't have to feel pressured into it. I can understand how you feel. Another time will be just fine."

He started to insist but realized that he should not push any further. He offered to cater to her desire and she declined, he was not going to pretend to be bothered by her indecisiveness. He opened her car door and helped her in. He told her that he would see her later in the week. After closing her door, he walked over to his own car and got in. He waited for her to pull off then he left the parking lot.

The drive home gave him time to think about how he would get Tammy to find out about Angelica.

CHAPTER

13

Dr. Painkin hurriedly raced to his office.

"Is there something wrong doctor?" Nurse Green questioned while watching the doctor entering his office in a hurry. She noted that he was perspiring with a wild, crazy look in his eyes. His hands trembled uncontrollably. She noticed that he was holding the Angelica Carty file in his hands and because of his obvious hysteria he was dropping portions of the file onto the floor.

"Dr. Painkin," she called again hoping to get his attention. When he didn't respond, she yelled out his name..."Steve!" Finally, her voice penetrated the wall built of fear." What's wrong?"

"I'm sorry Nurse Green; I just had something on my mind."

"I could see that, whatever it is, it's got you spooked."

"Have you seen Angelica's husband around here lately?"

"Yes, matter of fact, he was here earlier. He questioned some of the other nurses about her but the only thing everyone else knows is what's in her file...that she signed herself out and left. So you needn't worry, no one else knows of your relationship with her. How is she doing by the way?"

"Great!" Although he and Nurse Green were quite close, he didn't feel comfortable with her knowing that he was seeing Angelica.

"Listen, you've got to promise me that you will not let this spread through the hospital; especially when this guy is still asking questions about his wife. The last thing I need is to have a law suit slapped on me for misconduct and fraternizing with the patients."

"Of course, I would never do anything to hurt you. You have been there for me on many occasions and I'm not about to let you down now."

That was the thing that worried him the most. Nurse Green was known for gossiping. If there was any news to be gotten, she had it. She knew who was doing who and for how long and if there was anyone up next, she knew about that too. She didn't let anything get past her.

"Tracey, it is detrimental that you don't tell a soul about my relationship with this man's wife. Not only could I lose my job, I could lose my life as well. I've got a feeling that if he finds out that I'm dealing with his wife and I know that he already thinks it, he will definitely attempt to kill me."

"Well, the first thing, you need to do is not find yourself walking around with a discharged patient's file. It would seem you have a personal interest in her instead of a professional one. Once the patient is released from our care, whether it is with consent or not, you have to break all ties. There should be nothing that indicates that you have unprofessional feelings towards this patient including having her file, speaking with her husband or talking about her in general conversation."

"Thanks Tracey. I knew that I could count on you."

"That's Nurse Green around here. Now give me that file before you get yourself into trouble. By the way, were you able to get her into another facility?"

"Matter of fact, she didn't require any further treatment. All of her injuries were washed away as though it never happened."

"You don't say?"

"It's true. Tracey, I'm in love with her..."

He started to continue but there was someone standing at the door.

"May I help you Tammy?" he questioned attempting to hide his vexation. She paused for a moment wishing that she hadn't been caught standing there. In fact, she had been there for awhile listening to their conversation wondering if Sean's cousin was the woman who discharged herself from the hospital without telling anyone.

"Oh nothing, I was passing by and lost my train of thought. I'm sorry; I didn't mean to look like I was eaves dropping. I assure you, my mind was elsewhere."

She turned and walked away hoping that her shock wasn't evident. Nurse Green, which was the head nurse, followed behind her. Watching her every move to see what she was doing. About that time, the patient stress buzzer went off.

"Oh that's right, I was getting more gauzes for Mrs. Wannamaker's leg. I guess I took too long." Tammy spoke to herself aloud hoping that it would throw Nurse Green off her back. She looked down in a box under the cabinet and pulled out a few gauze packages and hurried past Nurse Green. She entered Mrs. Wannamaker's room and told her that it was time to change her dressing. She removed the bandages which were caked up with pus and blood, of course, it still wasn't time to change them but since she needed a decoy, she took the opportunity of making the patient more comfortable.

"Thank you, I was hoping that someone would come by soon to change them. The last hospital I was in, I had to fight with them to get my dressing changed. You see, I have diabetes and in order for this sore to heal, it needs to be cared for properly. You must be new around here because everyone else seems to be too busy for an old woman like myself!"

"No, it's just that things get a little hectic around here sometimes and everyone seems to be yelling for us simultaneously. Then we have other things that we are supposed to have done by a certain time. There are medications to be given and vitals to be taken for special care patients which cause other less critical patients to feel neglected. I'll try to see about you a little more frequently. How does that sound?"

"Wonderful. I appreciate that. I'll make certain that you get recognized for your kindness."

Tammy finished the dressing while talking to the patient, making her feel comfortable. Meanwhile, Nurse Green was standing left of the patient's room listening to the conversation seeing if she had indeed forgotten to get the dressing. When she had heard all that she wanted to hear, she returned to the office where Dr. Painkin was.

"So," he questioned her waiting for her findings...

"She was listening." Nurse Green confirmed.

"You've got to talk to her, tell her that this information must not be repeated."

"Don't worry, I'll keep her busy. In fact, I'll transfer her to another department so that she will never be able to run into him. She has information with no connection. So far, she was not around to meet him. I'll make certain that she never meets him. It will just be something that she will have to gossip about without any names or connection."

The doctor let out a sigh then got up to make his rounds. There were a few patients that were being prepped for surgery tomorrow and he wanted to answer any questions they might have today about it.

When the day finally ended, Dr. Painkin spoke to Nurse Green to see if she had taken care of Nurse Jacobsen. She told him that she didn't have a chance to talk to her but she will get to her later. Dr. Painkin left because he wanted to get an early jump home because tomorrow would be a long day and he was sure that Angelica was more than anxious to see him. He missed her when he had to work. He would make it up to her after that by taking her on a nice four week vacation. With all that has happened and him having to work the long hours that he did, they both deserved and needed the time to get to know each other. Dr. Painkin grabbed his jacket and told Nurse Green that he would be in early tomorrow morning. He had reviewed his charts and realized that he had four surgeries tomorrow; in fact, he would be booked solid for the next couple of weeks. He gave a sigh and prepared to go home where Angelica patiently waited for him.

Outside, the air was filled with the misty smog the earlier storm left behind. He hurried to his car expecting that rain could return any minute. He had a great deal on his mind and today was certainly not the kind of day he'd hoped for. In the car, he started the engine checking his mirrors. He realized that the defoggers needed a little help so he got out and wiped the windows and mirrors. Then returning to the car, he pulled out of the parking lot. He pulled out his Jesse Powell CD and put it into the player. A song he loved so well poured from the speakers... "Gloria". He sang the verses along with the soft music. It was the remix version. The song always reminded him of Angelica and what it

would be like without her in his life. He would certainly be lost. He looked into his rearview to see what
was behind him. He noticed a black sedan behind him
awfully close. He sped up a little bit and swore, wondering why people had to drive so close. He turned
onto the highway expecting that the car would have
kept straight but it didn't. He continued driving knowing that this guy was just going to be an asshole. After
exiting onto another expressway, he noticed that the
car still remained behind him and no matter how fast
he drove, the car maintained pace with him not allowing too much space to accumulate between them. He
wondered why the car was driving so close to him.
Then his mind went crazy. "Is this car following me?"
he wondered. Then he figured he was being paranoid.
With the events of the day, with that Ivan character, he
had no choice but to wonder if the man was crazy
enough to follow or attempt to intimidate him. He sped
up again now driving at seventy-five miles per hour zip-
ping in and out of traffics and forcing cars to gather
between them. The car fought to catch up with him.
He wondered if the guy was just trying to get around
him. He decided that he would get off at the next exit
to see if the car would follow him. When the exit came
up, he sped across two lanes and quickly exited not
leaving the other vehicle enough time to get off behind
him. He drove for about five minutes looking into his
rearview expecting to see him, but didn't. After a
while, he felt comfortable enough to get back onto the
expressway and that the car had to be far ahead of him
by now. He reentered half expecting to see the car.
When he didn't, he felt silly, thinking that someone
would not be crazy enough to follow him.

Taking a deep breath, he relaxed again. Then a few
exits ahead, he saw the same black sedan entering and

speeding up behind him. He tried to see who it was but couldn't because of the fog and mist. "Shit!", he cursed. "What does this guy want? The woman doesn't want him. Why can't he just realize that and leave us alone?" Steve remembered the grip Ivan had on his arm earlier. The man was definitely strong and would probably kill him, but for Angelica, he would gladly die trying to protect her. The car crazily bobbed and weaved through moving vehicles decreasing the distance between them. When there was no other cars between them, Steve attempted to see his assailant again, but couldn't. "Alright", he said, "you want me? Come and get me!" Steve sped to the far right lane expecting to get off at the next exit and handle the situation like a man. "Better now than never," he thought. Just as anticipated, the car followed him. When the exit came up, he got off and hurried to a nearby empty lot. He stopped the car in what seemed like the middle of nowhere. He reached into his glove compartment and grabbed his revolver. The moment he saw Ivan's face he would shoot it off unless he killed him first. He had purchased it right after he removed his Angel from the hospital. He would protect her even if it meant murder. If Ivan had a pact with her "till death do them part," then today would be that day. The car pulled just a few paces behind him. He wondered if his plea would hold up in court especially when it was over the man's wife. He also wondered would she defend him or would she cry over her abuser. He strained to see the person but couldn't. His window began to steam from his breath. It seemed an eternity waiting for him to arrive. That gave him the impression that he was probably waiting for his own doom. "Why did I leave the expressway anyway?" he asked himself. "Weren't you much safer there? You wouldn't be in this kind of trouble if you had only continued to drive. You could have led him right to the precinct or at least found a patrol car; they are always hiding somewhere looking for someone to pull over. But since I've chosen to make this my destiny, I guess that it will all end right here and Angelica will end up into the fire instead of the frying pan because if I kill him, I will go to jail and if he kills me, he will probably torture her worse than before until she finally dies." He shook the thought from his head. He would kill Ivan right here even if he has to die doing it. He waited more confident now for his tormentor to step to the car. When finally, the person stood at his door, he lowered the window holding the revolver pointed at the person but not in a way that he couldn't see it. A pair of black jeans stood there...Steve looked up expecting Ivan to be much quicker than himself since he wasn't used to this kind of thing and bring a crashing blow to his face knocking him unconscious and beating him to death. Not even giving him the dignity of turning his own weapon on him, allowing him to die like a man. He would be the bigger man in the end.

"Dr. Painkin!" Nurse Green shouted. "Why are you holding a gun at me? Do you know how long I have been trying to catch up with you? Why are you driving like a jackass anyway?"

"Nurse Green, what are you doing here?" He lowered the gun, placing it onto the seat next to him. "I thought you were someone else!"

"Well who did you think I was? And why do you want to kill them?"

"Never mind, why were you following me?"

"You left your wallet in the office and I thought you might need it. If I had known that I would be on a wild goose chase, I would have let you realize it on your own!"

Steve could feel himself sinking into the leather of his seat while she reprimanded him for being silly.

"I don't know what's going on with you but whatever it is, it's got you spooked and perhaps you should get rid of the problem!"

Her statement let him know that she knew exactly what was going on in his head. It had to do with him stealing that man's wife. He was certainly not going to go away quietly and Dr. Painkin was in for a fight; probably a fight to the death. Steve wondered if he could be that in love with her. Before he had time to tantalize that thought, another answered for him... "Yes! You do love her that much. Remember your promise." The voice in his head told him.

"I know Tracey. You don't need to tell me how stupid this is. Just try to understand that I have feelings for this woman, enough that I don't want to let her go. You mean to tell me that you have never run into anyone that made you feel that nothing else had purpose without them? Well?"

He waited for her to respond, when he received no response, he continued...

"Well that's how she makes me feel. I am in love with her and I don't know why. There's just this connection we have and everything just seems to be right between us. I don't think she came to me by accident. Someone or something wanted us to get together.

"No, that's just your dick talking!"

"No, it's not my dick talking. That woman should be dead right now. You saw the way she came to us. She had acute cerebral damage which I or no one else could have repaired. The woman's injuries are untraceable now. That didn't just occur. Something else gave her to me. Now it's my duty to love and take

care of her. Maybe it was taking her away from him.
In fact, he probably should never have known that she
made it through surgery. That was my mistake. I
know that now and that's why I'm having these problems. But in time, all that will be dealt with. So, don't
give me that man thinking with his dick line."

She looked at him realizing that he was sincere
about what he was saying. Although she didn't believe
any of it, she sympathized with him and wished him
the best.

"Listen, you had better be getting home, Angelica is
waiting for you. She's probably getting worried."

Steve looked at his watch and realized that it was
definitely getting late. It was now nine o'clock. Dr.
Painkin held her hand, looking up at her with eyes
filled with thanks and appreciation. He needed someone's understanding of the situation and she gave him
what he needed.

"Thanks Tracey."

"Listen, when love is involved, there is no right or
wrong answer. You just be careful. I don't want anything happening to you, okay?"

"I'll do my best. I imagine when it's all over someone will be hurt and I hope it's not me and especially
not Angelica."

Tracey returned to her car and Dr. Painkin walked
her to her vehicle. Steve knew behind that iron clad
attitude that she had a heart of gold. Even the mean-
est person has a soft spot. Steve watched her pull off
and he hurried to his car and followed her out of the lot
and back on to the highway. Nurse Green looked at
her watch and noticed that it was fifteen minutes past
nine o'clock and decided that it didn't make sense to
return to the hospital to finish up two hours. By the
time she got there it would be only another hour and a

half. She was only fifteen minutes to her house. Why would she make another trip this way when she was already there?

Steve got back onto the express way and headed for home. The surprises never seemed to end. First he runs into Ivan at the hospital and he questions him about his wife in an almost forceful manner. Then one of the new nurses overhears the conversation he has with Nurse Green about his relationship with Angelica and now he thinks that Ivan was following him and it turns out to be just Nurse Green. "What next?" He wondered.

Upon arriving home, he opened the door expecting yet another catastrophe but finding only Angelica who upon seeing her pushed the door closed and began to make love to her right at the door.

CHAPTER
14

Tammy looked at her watch - nine thirty - time had certainly gone by fast especially when something so critical was about to happen. She began to summarize the events of the day - "Sean's missing cousin was moved from the hospital by Dr. Painkin and for some reason they were trying to cover it up." She wondered if it was kidnap or did she leave on her own free will. "None the less, he has the right to know where his cousin was and how she's doing, right?" She wondered, "Is this something I should be staying out of. Why would Nurse Green go out of her way to keep this from me? There's got to be more to this than what I heard." She put on her coat and headed for the parking lot to pick up her car. She hated walking to the rear of the lot since it was dark back there. Not to mention, the rain and fog which makes it more difficult to see anything or anybody. She peered out the door wishing that she could blow the fog away. She waved at the security guard at the door and told him that she would see him in the morning. She had to do a double tomorrow.

"Listen, we can't get enough of you! Besides, who else takes care of the patients like you do?" The security guard replied back.

"Right," she said while leaving the hospital.

She started walking towards the parking lot when Ivan pulled up. The sight of him startled her. "Sean, what brings you here?"

"Surprised to see me huh?"

Her expression alone told him that she was holding something from him. She wasn't certain if telling him was a good idea yet. It's funny how a person's demeanor tells a great deal about them.

"What's on your mind?" he pressed, hoping that she would make it easier on him. Ivan was about tired of the games and she had better tell him what he needed to know. His smile widened, easing the tension she aparently had.

"Huh, nothing. It's just been a hectic day for me. I almost lost my job today after a heated argument with the Head Nurse."

"I see. Want some company?"

"No. I think that this is one of those occasions when one needs to handle things on their own, but thanks anyway."

"Did you forget we had a date tonight?"

"No, but tonight is not a good night for me and I have to pull a double tomorrow."

"Okay, then allow me to escort you to your car."

Tammy thought about it for a moment. The offer was greatly needed since her car was at the end of the dark parking lot and with no security out there, anything could happen. In fact his very presence shows how insecure the premises are.

"Sure, I'd appreciate that."

Ivan expected her to accept since he saw her car at the end of the parking lot. They should have security for these helpless women who fall vulnerable to men like myself. He chuckled before he could catch himself.

"What are you laughing at?"

"Nothing, I just thought of something funny that happened earlier."

Tammy sat there staring out the window ahead until they reached her car. Ivan grabbed her head from behind and began kissing her passionately half expecting her to pull away, but she didn't. She welcomed it. Her hair felt like soft cotton between his fingers. Tammy tried desperately to ignore the tiny knot snagged in his fingernail but that dammed thing wouldn't pop or come free. "Sean?"

"I know you want to go home right?"

"No. You've got my hair caught in your fingernail."

"Oh, I'm sorry." He removed his hand and looked forward. Just the idea of him being clumsy embarrassed him. Tammy was about to get out of the car when he began to kiss her again. He was determined not to let her leave the car without erasing any insecurity she had developed about him. His lips softly caressed hers with his tongue dancing around hers. He placed her hand on his throbbing organ. She could feel his urgency and knew that something had to be done about it. This was definitely a different man since the last time. She presumed that he had gotten over that little insecurity that he had the last time. He unbuttoned her dress allowing it to fall open revealing a satiny white bra. Two nicely sized mountains were bound by a tiny hook in the center of her breasts. He freed them, watching them fall apart like a rockslide. He buried his head between them working his face around until he found the erected nipple which was hot against his lips. A sigh of delight escaped her lips as she massaged his scalp. He continued down until he met her furry mound.

"Don't you wear underwear?"

"Sometimes. Why do you prefer that I had some on right now?"

He didn't respond. Taking a whiff of her musky

squirrel filled his nostrils with pheromones. She wanted him and he knew it. His tongue swiped against her clitoris sending waves of pure pleasure through her, one behind the other. He continued to make her flow of passion generate. Meanwhile her hand fumbled with his raging bull which was ready to devour its target. Tammy went wild with passion as she pushed Ivan back so that she could take his fullness into her mouth, aggressively descending and ascending the length of his shaft, toying with the cables which coiled it. Sucking, bitting, licking, tasting, squeezing, stroking and loving him in ways he thought impossible. Intensity built rapidly as his blood began to boil. He forced her head down, working his hips in a circular motion causing her to take him a little deeper. While toying with her moist flesh and spreading her fluids around preparing for entrance, he only imagined what entering her was like, touching the tiny nodules that lined the walls of her vagina - "penile ticklers," he thought. She was tight enough to be considered new but of course, he knew she wasn't, however, it was good enough. He wanted so greatly to enter her, to make her scream his name and make fuck faces. She wanted him too because she pulled at him beckoning him to climb atop her and show her what he was made of.

"You want it?" he asked her as she raised her head.

"Give it to me daddy," she said welcoming him to the dance. He climbed atop her and was about to aggressively enter her when he saw someone coming.

"Damn," he swore while taking his place next to her in the driver's seat.

She looked back and saw that her co-worker Carol searching for her car through the fog mist. Carol saw her and came to see if everything was all right since

Tammy's car was still parked. She tapped on the window and Ivan lowered it so that she could talk to her friend. He kept his face turned revealing only his profile and hoping that she wouldn't recognize him. Tammy turned to Ivan with a disappointed look on her face. He was exhilarating and she wanted to finish what they started.

"Well, thanks Sean for giving me a lift to my car. I'll be fine now. Listen, perhaps we'll catch up with each other some other time."

He nodded in agreement while she exited his car. His member throbbed vehemently, realizing that it wasn't going to be fulfilled after being coaxed into this fury of emotion. He watched Carol disappear with Tammy to their cars. They talked for a few minutes and he waited to see if he noticed any change in her attitude. He would kill that bitch if she interfered or complicated the situation. They talked a few moments longer then Tammy got into her car and she waited to see Carol get into her car. When Carol was in her car, Tammy pulled off and exited the parking lot. Ivan already found a quiet spot to wait for Carol. Right outside the hospital grounds, Ivan waited about two blocks down. Carol exited the parking lot and waited at the corner for the light to change so that she could proceed. While waiting, she inserted her Phil Collins CD and began singing one of his classic tunes. The light changed and she sped down the street. Carol only lived about fifteen minutes from the hospital so her traveling time was quite short. She didn't notice the car driving behind her. Nothing existed in her world except her, Phil Collins and the road. She was supposed to work late tonight but one of the other nurses covered for her. She couldn't take another long night. For the past two, she had been working doubles and five hours overtime.

Finally, she pulled onto her driveway and used her remote to open her garage. When it opened, she drove the car into it, still remaining there listening to the rest of her favorite song. Ivan lurked through the shadows rapidly nearing her car. He could see that silly wench sitting in the car instead of going into the house and locking the door. *Didn't she know that no neighborhood was safe at night?* shaking his head. Finally, the song ended and she could take out her CD and turn off the motor. She opened the door and Ivan stood in front of her. The sight of him brought trepidation. She had just told Tammy that she should stay away from him because he was crazy. She wanted to tell her more but Tammy dismissed anything she had to say. She figured that it was office gossip. Besides, she never saw him around the hospital anyway.

"Mr. Carty?"

"So you even remembered my name. If you know that much, you must know why I'm here!"

"No I don't."

A crashing blow descended upon her face forcing her back into the car. Since she had already locked the garage door, no one could see inside. She was too afraid to scream. She was hoping that whatever he wanted he would take it and leave.

"So tell me, Carol, do you now remember where my wife went?" His eyes glared at her, twinkling in the darkness. He pulled her from the car and leaned her against the car pressing his body tightly against hers.

"You're not going to rape me are you?"

"Would you like me to?"

She shook her head in response..."No".

"Then why would I do that? I'm no rapist! I don't take anything which isn't given to me."

A feeling of relief befell her. Maybe he wouldn't kill her either.

"So back to my question. Where is my wife?"

"I told you what I knew about the situation that day you were at the hospital asking questions."

He struck her again..."No, that was a little stage show you and Nurse Green conjured up for me. I want the truth now!"

"That was the truth. Angelica Carty signed herself out that night and the papers were given to her by..."

She hesitated; searching for the nurse that handled the situation...

"I don't know who gave her the papers, but Nurse Green would. Once I told her that she had to wait for Dr. Painkin, she was adamant on leaving and that's exactly what she did."

"Okay, then what did she have on when she left?"

"Blue jeans and a red sweater." Ivan thought about it and realized that she didn't come there dressed in jeans. He expected her to tell him that she left with the hospital clothes. He had taken her clothes home with him when he left.

"Where did the clothes come from?"

"I don't know, all I know is what she had on when she came to the station."

Her eyes said that she was lying. She knew exactly where Angelica was or at least who would know. She definitely didn't walk out on her own accord and someone was helping her, encouraging her.

"What about Nurse Green?"

Carol looked dumbfounded.

"What about Nurse Green?"

"She seems to be pretty close with Dr. Painkin, perhaps she knows something?"

"How would I know what's in her head."

Ivan rested his hand against her larynx without applying any pressure, warning her that another statement like that one would earn a squeeze.

"Are you sure you couldn't speculate?"

"Listen, all I know is that your wife signed herself out. Any politics that goes on in that hospital is far from my knowledge. I don't have any pull in the hospital and certainly wouldn't know of any personal going ons of Dr. Painkin or Nurse Green. Probably you should ask her if you want further answers!"

"Fine, I'll do that!" he said with his hand remaining around her throat. He watched her fear stricken eyes. He knew that she anticipated his next move. She remembered something someone told her a long time ago "Anticipation of death is worst than death itself!" As many times as she'd heard it, never had that phrase held any meaning until now.

"So what happens to me now?" she asked realizing that this was her moment of judgement.

"The Grim Riper has come to visit you and to tell you that your presence on this Earth is no longer needed." His casual tone frightened her and it had nothing to do with the fact that she was about to die but how! Waiting was the hardest thing and worst than that, she didn't think he knew how he was going to kill her. Looking into his eyes, she could see that there was no animosity and his killing her was purely out of necessity.

"I know you don't want to kill me and that you're only doing it because you have to so whatever you do just make it..."

With a quick twist, he broke her neck. A slight drizzle of blood trickled down her lip. Her eyes stared up at him, thanking him for making it quick. A look of peace shone on her face as her still eyes gazed through the roof of her car into the heavens.

Ivan knew what had to be done next. He closed the car door and exited the garage. The stillness of the night still remained. Not a peeping neighbor was to be seen neither a passing car. *Nice neighborhood*, he thought while returning to his car. In the center of the street's tranquility, Ivan thought he saw a shadow standing there watching him. He squinted to gain clarity but it was gone. He walked in its direction and still, nothing. Peering through a linden of trees, Ivan continued his search for his watcher. Whoever it was, they escaped quietly. Shrugging, he returned to his car, half expecting to see someone looking out at him but didn't.

"In all good time, in all good time." The Shadow said watching Ivan get away with yet another life.

CHAPTER

15

Officer Brown called the two officers watching the Givens place to give them the order to pick up Mr. Davis.

"Thompson here."

"Thompson, bring him in we've got a DOA at Twin Pine Drive, another unfortunate involved with our innocent Mr. Davis...not to mention a key witness who is willing to testify that he was seeing her and handled her pretty roughly. She's positive that he's our guy."

"What's the charge?"

"Murder."

"Mr. Davis just left the Givens place and he was having a discussion with a gentleman by the name of Ivan. He claims that Ivan killed Ms. Givens."

"What response did this Ivan guy give?"

"He didn't. In fact, the statement kind of amused him. I think this Ivan character is kind of shady. His nonchalance doesn't seem to fit the scenario. I think we need to get him in here for questioning too."

"No, I think we've got our man. This Rich guy seems to have a thing for strangling women. I don't think it's a coincidence that this Rich character was also involved with the girl we found today."

"We're expecting that he will return tonight to the Givens place and we'll pick him up then."

Officer Thompson radioed the surveillance team and told them that they no longer needed to keep an eye on Ivan.

"Thompson, this is Garrison, I've got Ivan here at the St. Agnes Hospital. He just picked up a woman and they're headed through the parking lot."

"We've found another body linked to Mr. Davis. Strangled just like the first one only thing, this time there was no struggle so no blow was needed."

"Okay, we're leaving the premises now. Meet you back at the station."

The officers looked at each other. Although they had a bad feeling about Ivan, surveillance ceased and they left from their parked area and headed for the station.

❧⍤❧

Richard had gone to Ivan's house to see if he could find anything that would divert the attention from him for awhile, at least long enough for Ivan to reveal his true colors. He strummed through papers, scrutinized pictures and other personal items. He noticed a marriage certificate which validated that Ivan did indeed have a wife. He also noticed that she was young. He searched for a picture of her. He found one, she was absolutely beautiful. Her eyes were grey with what appeared to be green accents. She had sandy brown hair with natural blonde accents. Bob definitely had nothing on this chick.

He moved on to their wardrobe which contained cute little dresses which belonged to Ivan's wife. Rich looked at the tag - size 10. He imagined that she had a nice rear with shapely thighs which was a trademark of black women. Everything proportioned to perfection. No matter what size they were, shape was something they would always be blessed with. The thought of Ivan's wife's body made him think of Geneva, who was probably home wondering why he hadn't come by.

She was a nice piece of work herself, sometimes she got a little out of hand and he had to show her who wore the pants in the relationship but ultimately, she was a pretty nice girl.

He looked at his watch and realized that he had better be getting out of Ivan's house. Certainly, he would be walking in at any moment and that would cause more problems than he wanted to deal with. Rich had been rambling through Ivan's belonging for over two hours and found nothing incriminating. There was nothing that said that he was violent or even messed around. He had a lovely wife whose face was remarkable in every picture that he looked at. Maybe the Bob situation was an isolated incident and there was nothing that could place him at the scene. Rich worried that he was probably going to take the full rap for the murder of Barbara Givens and there was no way out of it. The fact of the matter was that Ivan had practically killed her when he got there he just finished her off instead of helping her.

"There's got to be something that will point a finger or at least raise an eyebrow about him. No one is perfectly clean. There's some dirt on everyone. Not even a lily is pure white. I'm just looking in the wrong place." "If I wanted to hide something, where would I put it?" He stood in the center of the room looking around as though he expected some piece of evidence to stand out. His watchful eyes scanned the room. It was something about the way the mattress not being aligned properly that just didn't rub him the right way. He walked over to it. He looked at his surroundings and everything seemed to be in order and neatly placed. "Why was the mattress misaligned?" He wondered. He looked under the pillow and felt the casing to see if perhaps there was something in it... nothing.

He slid his hand under the mattress feeling for anything that might have been placed under it...nothing.
He went over to the other side where he imagined his
wife must sleep and felt under the mattress...nothing.
Then to the foot of the bed...finally he felt something.
He worked his hand around to get a good feel of it. He
couldn't find the edges but it felt hard. He lifted the
mattress slightly so that he could get his hand around
it...WHAP

"SHIT!" He screamed while snatching his hand
from under the mattress to find that his finger was
hanging by a thread with a special mouse trap still
hanging to a sliver of flesh. Cursing beneath his breath
he examined the gadget. The thing reminded him of a
guillotine - instead of a heavy wire slamming across his
finger; it was a very sharp blade, well more like a
scalpel. "That bastard, why the fuck would he put
something under his bed like that? Shit! Shit! Shit!"

Ivan had filed the spring-action wire of a mouse-
trap so fine that it cut like a blade. Blood shot from his
finger. He was bleeding all over the covers. "Damn,
this is all I need; breaking in and entering. "What is he
protecting under there that he would go through such
desperate measures to protect?" He lifted the mattress
ever higher this time but the covers prevented him
from seeing anything. His hand throbbed with pain.

"Fuck it!" He cursed and threw the mattress to the
side so that he wouldn't run into any other surprises...still nothing. This didn't make any sense. "I know
he didn't do this just for the hell of it, and it certainly
wasn't meant for his wife. What does he have rats that
sneak up under his mattress big as dogs?" He looked
at the empty box spring and knew that there was
something he wasn't seeing and he wasn't about to lose
his finger over nothing. He knelt and looked under the

bed...nothing. "What the fuck is he hiding? This guy must be out of his fucking mind to do something like this when there's nothing to be found."

He looked at his finger again. It was beginning to turn blue.

"Damn! I'd better get my ass to the emergency room and have this taken care of before I bleed to death!" He started to replace the mattress and realized that it didn't make any sense since he had bled all over the place anyway. "He would certainly know that someone had been to his place. I imagine that he would think it was the police investigating him."

When he had reached his car, he realized that this was the kind of evidence he needed to prove that Ivan was sick and definitely capable of murder. "Why would a married man put something so wicked under the mattress where he and his wife sleep unless there was something he didn't want her to see and would punish her just for looking. The clever bastard probably expected someone to look under the mattress so he set a booby-trap there so that he would know that someone was looking for something." Rich started the engine and realized that although this was the perfect thing to bring to the police, he had no right breaking into Ivan's house. "Fuck me! I can't win for losing!"

He hurried to the nearest hospital so that someone could take a look at his hand and hopefully save his index finder. Not to mention close up the gash that went across the rest of his fingers. The shock from seeing his index finger dangling from his hand that way made him not notice the injury the rest of his fingers sustained. He would get Ivan for this.

෴

Officer Thompson waited as long as he could for

Rich to return to the Given's place. They looked at the clock and it was two o'clock in the morning.

"Do you think he's still coming back here tonight?"

"I doubt it. It's getting late and I for one would like to get home to my wife."

"So radio it in and have someone else come and watch for him. But I've got a feeling that he won't be returning here tonight."

"Well, we're supposed to bring him in so perhaps we should be going to his place to pick him up."

"Let's do it. There's no need in us sitting here waiting for him when we've got the order to pick him up." Thompson started the car and slowly drove away from the elaborate home of Barbara Givens.

"You're right. It just would have been better to have something concrete in hand when we bring him before the judge."

"Yeah, well sometimes things just don't work out that way."

"I think they're making a mistake. Something just doesn't seem right about this."

"Since when did you start being a detective?"

"Since this whole thing started. I believe this Rich character had something to do with these deaths and probably he did commit them, however, I think that Ivan is in on it too."

"You're probably right, but I'm sure he'd come out squeaky clean so there's no need in entertaining it." Thompson gave a quick look of surprise at his partner who never had anything to say. For once, he opposed something. "Are you taking this case personal?"

"No. I just for once want to see the law prevail and I think that there's more to this picture than the murder of Barbara Givens and this girl on Twin Pine Drive."

"I think so too. I wonder if this Ivan character knew

her as well."

"So do you want to do some checking around? We can start by asking people at her job, the neighbors, and friends to see if anyone recognized him or knew of their acquaintance."

"Well you know that we require clearance and there's no way Brown is going to give it to us." They pulled in front of Mr. Davis' house. All the lights were out and there was no car in the driveway. "So what do you think?"

"That he's not here."

"Want to check the house anyway?"

"No need, there's no one here. If he was in there, his car would be in the driveway."

"Perhaps he doesn't want anyone to know he's home."

"Nah, trust me, he's not in there. This character is out on his killing spree or hiding out."

"So back to the station?"

"You got it." Thompson could see that his partner didn't want to let this thing go. Tonight was going to be one of those detective nights and he was going to figure this thing out if it killed him. "Listen, I can see that you're not satisfied with returning to the station so what do you suggest we do?"

"How about we see if Ivan's home? Perhaps Rich decided to pay Ivan a visit and that was his cue when they had their discussion earlier!"

"It's a long shot but what the hell."

Thompson, like his partner had the same feeling that something was wrong and checking out Ivan was a good start. Luckily for them the drive was only thirty minutes because Thompson didn't think he could take a long drive. They pulled in front of Ivan's house. Everything was quiet. He just didn't seem the country

type. Houses were spaced out and private. Trees surrounded the premises. "The guy didn't strike me as the
nature type."

"Well, seems to me he prides tranquility and privacy."

"He should certainly get a lot of that out here."

They turned off the engine leaving the headlights
on.

"No car in the driveway, you think he's out also?"

"They must be at the same party."

At the door, the porch was stained with droplets of
blood. Thompson bent down to touch it.

"Still wet."

"Fresh." Withdrawing their weapons, Thompson
waved his gun gesturing his partner to step aside. Two
shots were fired tearing holes through the hinges and
with a swift kick, the door fell in. Thompson with his
partner a few paces behind cautiously moved through
the house, searching for either a dead body or some
explanation for the blood on the porch.

Searching the kitchen, they could see no one was in
there. Banner was glad this was a single level house.
He hated searches where the perpetrator had an
advantage. Working their way to the rear rooms,
droplets of blood glistened in the darkness like black
diamonds. The bedroom door was opened. Banner
peeked in with Thompson ready to fire. He waved his
hand to tell him that he could lower his gun. There
was no one in the house. Someone had destroyed the
room. Papers were everywhere, drawers pulled from
the chest of drawers, broken as though someone threw
them. The mattress had also been thrown to the side.

"Ivan must have gone plum crazy in here. What do
you think happened?"

"I'm not sure."

Thompson flashed his light around the room until he spotted the light switch. When he turned the light on, he could see that someone must have been looking for something in a hurry.

"Well, one thing, it rules out Ivan. I'm sure whatever he was looking for wouldn't have been that important that he would ransack his own house."

"So who do you think did it?"

The officers walked deeper into the room and noticed more blood which seemed to start on the boxspring.

"What the fuck happened here. He looked to see if there was something sharp protruding from the bedspring but found none. He searched the floor and under the bed...just beneath the bed he saw what must have been the cause for all the blood shed...he began to laugh uncontrollably.

"Come take a look at this," he called to his partner who was now looking through the papers that were thrown on the floor surrounding the nightstand, gesturing for him to hurry. Thompson hurried over to get a look at what Banner had found...

"Now this is the act of a crazy son-of-a-bitch. No one in their right mind would have something like this laying around."

"Maybe he didn't have it laying around. Maybe he hurt himself trying to set it up."

"No, I think someone else found this little contraption. Ivan would not have fallen into his own trap. At least not something like this."

Banner scratched his head.

"This doesn't make any sense. Why would he have something like this in the house anyway? Do you think it was under the bed all the time? Or did it end up here?"

I think that if it was under the bed, he expected that someone would have been looking under there for something. Could you imagine coming in and finding a rat's head cut off under your bed?"

"No, but this was no rat and it happened recently. Look, the blood's still thin." Simultaneously they said…"To the hospital."

"So, I presume the injury over the last two hours must be severed fingers," Banner couldn't hold his laugh any longer.

"That's right."

"Damn, you would think the guy would have sense enough to look before he stuck his hand under there." Another outburst of laughter followed. They turned off the lights and headed for St. Agnes Hospital which was the nearest to the residence.

৵৶

Ivan had to find out how much Tammy knew about him. The night seemed longer than any other he had known. He recollected the doctor's response when he mentioned his wife. The nerve of him to try to hide what he was doing and pretend he didn't know who she was when the guilt showed clearly on his face. Then the damn Nurse Green who thinks she's got the whole thing under control is only sealing her fate. Ivan gritted his teeth loathing her for what she was doing. "Doesn't anyone have principals anymore? I'll kill her for her involvement in all this." He could see Angelica's beautiful grey eyes looking lovingly up at him while he made love to her. Behind each kiss, she would slowly blink with an even greater look of enjoyment when her irises reappeared. Her teeth were bright and glistened in the darkness from the moon's light while she smiled at him. She loved him so much, tolerating his many mood swings. He reached out to draw her near to him when Dr. Painkin snatched her away. He cradled her in his arms and passionately kissed her while Ivan could do nothing but watch. He could feel the anger building inside him. "Angelica," he called out to her wishing that she would turn to him but she didn't. She said she would never return to him. Then another person appeared, it was his mother reminding him that he would be just like his father. "Your father was never good for anything other than beating on a woman. That's what killed him. That's what will kill you." Then he remembered sitting watching his father pouring down his fury over his mother's head until she would lay still and lifeless. But when she regained consciousness, she would love him just the same, even more in fact, until one day she just couldn't take it any more. When his father came in from work, smelling of sweet perfume and preparing to lash out at his mom she pulled out a gun and shot him three times in the chest. He remembered the words his father used to tell him..."Son, never let a woman rule you and never let them walk away." Those words echoed in his memory while he remembered his father staggering over to his mother, falling and tripping over furniture and her struggle to get away from him. Even with three bullets in his chest, he still had enough energy to do what was necessary to keep her from leaving him. When he had finally caught her, he snatched the gun from her and threw it to the floor. He placed his large hands around her throat. Ivan's dad was six foot four inches tall with a forty-eight inch back and narrow waist. He was a very largely built man and well put together. He spent hours in the gym sculpturing his body and making his already formidable size more intimidating which only added to his handsome features. Ivan guessed that's what always got him in trouble - the women found him irresistible and he didn't attempt to resist them either. Whenever his mother questioned him about it, he would answer her with a blow - subject closed. His father with blood pouring profusely from his chest wrapped one arm around his wife's neck with the other around her waist. She struggled to get away from him. He guessed in the end, he still loved her while he squeezed the last breath of air from her body. The two of them fell to the floor cradled in each other's arms and that's how the police found them.

Then Ivan saw Angelica standing cradled in another man's arms. He warned her that he would never let her go. She would not leave him. She, like his parents, would die in his arms. They would spend their eternity together - if they were Hell bound, he would hold her while Lucifer's flames swept the very flesh from their bones or if Heaven be their destiny, he would be there to cleanse her pearly white wings and like the God of love, he would spend eternity loving her. But nothing would separate them from each other.

He pulled in front of Tammy's house. There was a light still on in what he presumed to be her bedroom. He walked through her grass and peeped through the window. She was laying on the bed with the covers covering only her legs. Her back and head were propped up by pillows while she held a book up in front of her reading intently. Most of the pages were to the right side so he could tell that she was at the height of the book which explained why she would be sitting up so late trying to read when she had to get up early to go to work. He walked to the door and rung the bell.

Tammy looked at her clock...ten thirty.

"I wonder who that could be this late at night."

She grabbed her robe and went to the door. She looked out and saw Sean standing there. She opened the door quickly and invited him in.

"What brings you to my door?"

Ivan's eyes searched hers to see if there was anything faulty in them but instead, he saw only urgent desire and longing. He placed his hand around her waist and pulled her to him. She released her robe and let it fall open revealing her sheer night gown. Her arms found their way around his waist as well. He lowered his lips to meet hers. Tammy was exceptionally tall for a woman. She was six feet tall and Ivan wasn't used to tall women. Usually, he would lift them up to meet his lips while standing but she had no difficulty reaching his lips, in fact, her arms wrapped around his neck. Her breasts were ripe and ready for picking as he felt her hardened nipples pressed against his chest.

She pulled away from him holding his hand while leading him to the living room. As much as she wanted him, she needed to ask him some questions and the information she learned earlier, she felt that he had a right to know what happened to his cousin. Carol was trying to tell her something about him but she said she would call later since he was right there. When they had reached the living room, Ivan waited in anticipation. He knew that there was something on her mind besides exploring his body. Probably it was the same thing that was on her mind earlier when he met her in front of the hospital. She searched his eyes hoping to receive some form of truth and honesty. He didn't have anything malicious going on in there. Ivan's eyes were indeed sincere and his concern for whatever she wanted to ask was evident.

"Sean, you know when I told you earlier that I had an argument with the head nurse and I was still a little shaken about it?"

Ivan shook his head and he listened more intently,

waiting for what he knew would be the answer to what he wanted to know.

"Well, Nurse Green was talking about your cousin who left the hospital." Excitement and concern came to Ivan's eyes.

"What did they say? Is she alright?"

"Yes, apparently, she did indeed leave on her own accord and no one forced her to leave, so you can scratch that one off the list."

"So where is she?"

"I'm not sure, but my guesstimate and recommendation would be to ask Nurse Green about it because she seems to know exactly where she is."

"Did they say anything else?"

"No, because they noticed me standing outside the door and they stopped speaking. Nurse Green seemed very angry about finding me there but I convinced her that I was only looking for some materials and not eavesdropping. She kept a close eye on me for the rest of the day and I tried to avoid her so that she wouldn't think anything about me being there. Sean, I will probably lose my job over this but if it helps you rekindle your relationship with your cousin and bring peace of mind to your family, it was well worth it."

"Thanks Tammy. You don't find people willing to go out of their way for someone else with nothing to gain everyday. But I want to ask you another question."

"Anything. What is it?"

"You mentioned they, who was she speaking to?"

"Oh, I'm not sure but I think it was Dr. Painkin."

He grabbed her face and showered her with kisses because she confirmed what he suspected. Now he would find Nurse Green because she would point him in the direction of Dr. Painkin.

"I'm sorry I didn't hear any more, but they were

awfully hush hush about it."

"Did you hear anything about Dr. Painkin having a relationship with her?"

"No. I didn't hear anything like that. They were just mentioning that she was married to a man who was beating on her and almost killed her."

"Yeah, she did have a little domestic problem but we were prepared to handle the situation but she took matters into her own hands and now no one can help her. She made matters worse running away like that."

"What do you mean? If the guy was beating on her, and doesn't know where she is, maybe she's safe where she is."

"No, he could be looking for her and in great danger. I want to get to her first before she does something crazy."

Tammy now wondered what Carol wanted to tell her about him. Sean should certainly know where this man lived and be capable of making him leave his cousin alone. Its not often you find a cousin searching for his relative as diligently as this man is looking. Tammy leaned over and kissed Ivan's lips...

"I'll be right back so don't run away okay?"

"I won't go anywhere."

Tammy went to the back and dialed Carol's number. The phone only rang. Carol certainly shouldn't be sleep this soon. Carol was not the type of person who went home and went straight to bed. "Perhaps she's taking a nice long bath; I'll try her back later."

When she turned around, Ivan was standing behind her. The sight of him frightened her.

"Hi, got impatient huh? I was coming back, I just wanted to call a friend before I forgot, and I know the minute we get started, I wouldn't be thinking about anything else."

"Is that right?"

"Yeah."

Her lips met his again while watching his curious eyes. She could tell he didn't believe her and the frightening thing about it is that he didn't seem to care. Whatever his plans were, he was going to carry them out despite anyone. Tammy could feel his erection building as her tongue wrestled with his. She pushed him backward onto her bed and he allowed himself to fall at her will. She straddled over him while wrestling with his belt. She unbuttoned his pants and slowly rolled the zipper down. He had boxers on which through the hole, she could see dark strands of hair. She reached in and grabbed his instrument of passion massaging it with her palms and clasped hands. Ivan watched her while she toyed with him.

One thing he had to respect, she was not the kind of lady to lose her cool when she was uncertain about something. This situation was definitely making her uncomfortable but she wanted him and no matter what, she was going to have him before she revealed it. *That takes guts*, he thought.

She lowered her lips to it and like a Blow Pop, began to suck.

"Oh my God!" Ivan exclaimed. "You are absolutely beautiful. Mmmm, suck it. Who taught you to do that? Huh? Who taught you to please a man like this?" She continued to do him because she enjoyed the sound of his voice talking dirty to her. The sound of lips smacking, slobbering and puffing filled the room like an orchestra of concupiscence as Tammy moved her mouth up and down his shaft, sweeping her tongue over, under and around his slimy head.

"Ooooh," he crooned in his deep voice while forcing her to take it a little deeper. She pulled his pants from under his butt and down his legs and over his feet. Then she did the same with his boxers. His dick slapped his stomach when she pulled his underwear down. She told him to spread his legs like a bitch so she could lick his balls - and he did. Her tongue moved from side to side between his balls. She pulled them one at a time into her mouth. "You like that baby?"

"Oh yeah."

"Turn over." He did exactly what she told him to and she spread his cheeks apart and placed her tongue to the entrance of his anus and she forced her tongue into it, working it around and around, in and out. Ivan had never felt anything in his ass before and realized that he liked it. She used one hand to massage his shaft while caressing the head of his penis and using her middle finger to gently move in and out of his rectum. He tightened up preparing to make her stop but she held his thighs and told him to enjoy it. She masturbated him while biting and sucking at his thighs and knees. He twitched at each touch. She straddled over his face placing her pussy over his mouth moving in a fucking motion.

"Fuck me with your tongue. Make me come in your face."

Ivan grabbed her buttocks and pulled her down to his face and forced his tongue into her. His tongue was long and wet. It moved in and out rapidly causing her to tremble. She worked her pussy as his tongue toyed with her growing pearl. She forced his nose to stoke her hole. The bony, point of his nose felt good, it was like fucking a real dick.

"Holy crap!" she exclaimed as the white lava shot from his body and into her face like Nickelodeon Gak. She used it to massage him. She felt an orgasm nearing and pressed her fat ass down onto his face almost suffocating him. Ivan quickly flipped her onto the bed and off his face before she burned a hole in it. He used his cum as a lubricant then gently pressed his sensitive organ into her ass. She had done it before and he knew it because unless a woman's been taught, they don't know how to do the dirty things this woman was doing. The resistance was slight as he penetrated her. Her hands gripped the sheets as she strained to adjust to his size. He had been blessed but it didn't feel like a blessing at the moment. Ivan sensed her discomfort and forced his hands underneath her so that he could toy with her. She began to relax and finally experience the pleasure of being fucked in the ass.

"Tell me, do you like it like this?"

"I like it anyway you want to do it big fellow."

"You know I would have never expected this type of behavior from you."

"I know, but had I shown it to you initially, would you have wanted it? Respected it?"

"Probably not, but what makes you think I do now?"

"You do. I have no doubt."

Her head remained faced down because she was confident that his feelings remained in tact. Then came the question she didn't expect...

"So now that you know I'm Angelica's husband, will you help me find her?"

"How did you know that I figured it out?"

"I figured you knew since your conversation with your co-worker Carol."

"I see. So what made you think she told me anything? The truth of the matter is she wanted to tell me something but didn't want to talk right then. She said it had something to do with you. At first, I thought that she knew you from somewhere else, but when I tried to call her and no one answered her phone, I knew that something had to be wrong and with you sneaking up behind me the way you did, I knew that you must have been the husband that has been looking for his wife. So why did you lie to me in the first place instead of telling me the truth?"

"I didn't want to kill you."

"Thanks. I'm really not ready to die and yes, I will help you if you promise to come back to me. You know that if she has indeed run away with the doctor that she has no intention of returning to you, right?"

"I know, but I can't let him have her either and I must give her the benefit of the doubt. My angel would not leave on her own accord; he's feeding her false promises. He can't protect her."

Ivan withdrew himself and inserted it into her vagina. While pulling her hair, he rapidly pounded his member into her bringing her to the supplicating climax she awaited. As her pussy collapsed to the sheets, he admired her bravery. She was made for him. He hated a wimp, there was no way he could kill her. He took a position next to her and she looked into his eyes...

"So, now that I know your name isn't Sean and your plot has been revealed, tell me, what's your real name?"

"Ivan Carty."

"Nice to meet you Ivan Carty. So, is Carol dead?"

"Yes, I had no choice but to kill her. She would have ruined my plans. She would not have volunteered to help me or keep quiet, so I silenced her."

"Did you fuck her too?"

Ivan laughed; he couldn't believe this woman was feeling jealous after all he just did for her.

"No, she didn't want it, she asked me if I was going

to rape her and I told her that I didn't take anything thing that wasn't given to me and she didn't offer."

"At least you're polite about it. So, what now?"

"I need to find out how to reach Nurse Green. Do you have any idea where she lives?"

"No, but when I go to the office tomorrow, I will be happy to go through the files and see if I can get it for you."

He kissed her.

"I'm glad we met, I knew there was something special about you. Those innocent eyes are really becoming."

"Why thank you, it's the look of sin."

"I know."

He held her close to him and closed his eyes. Not long after that, she closed her eyes as well. Sleep that night was sweet. Her dark angel had come to her and she would do everything she could to make him happy. *Angelica was a fool to think she could escape him and now she would die and Ivan would belong to me alone.*

She remembered how her husband thought he could walk away from their marriage and live happily ever after with another woman. When they woke up, they were both surprised to see that the death angel was visiting them. She had come to clean up the mess they had caused by pouring sulphuric acid over them and watching until there was nothing left, not even their bones or the bed they were laying in. She wondered what Ivan would do when he found his beautiful Angelica and the good doctor. It would take an act of God to save her and he wouldn't dare to intervene because he said "what he has yoked together, let no man put asunder".

CHAPTER
16

Rich was out of surgery. The doctor told him that he had gotten there just in time to save the nerves in his fingers. There was limited damage done and the injury was treatable. Of course, his hand hurt like hell despite the pain killers that were given to him. Still groggy from the anesthesia he attempted to pull his arm up so that he could get a look at his hand.

"What the fuck?" he said realizing that he had been cuffed to the railing. Officers Thompson and Banner had already questioned and reviewed the cases that had come in last night and as suspected, a familiar name popped up. They placed him under arrest and made certain that he would not try to leave when he awakened. Rich presumed that Ivan, after finding his home vandalized, called the police and reported it. Rich had given him just the tool needed to spread the icing on the cake. Now he would have trouble explaining why he was at Carty's residence. "How the hell did he know," Rich wondered. As obvious as it seemed, Rich had to assume that Ivan was by far too cleaver for that. He would have a better plot for him. "What the hell I might as well try and get some rest as my buddy officers will be here soon to question me and by then, I had better have an answer or explanation." Looking out the window, Rich presumed that it had to be about seven o'clock in the morning. It wasn't like the law to keep a guy waiting.

He felt the urge to go to the bathroom and started urinating uncontrollably,   expecting to feel wet but didn't. He sat up on the bed to see that there was a tube jammed up the tiny hole in his penis aiding him where he didn't require aid.

"Good morning Mr. Davis, I'm sure that you must have realized by now that you have been placed under arrest sometime during the night. The officers will be here in just a little bit to tell you what's going on. In the meantime, how are you feeling?"

"How the hell do you think I'm feeling? I came here for help and you guys call the police on me. I didn't do anything wrong. I told you that it was an accident."

"Oh no Mr. Davis, the officers came looking for you. In fact, they were looking for someone with injuries just like your own and when they came across your name, they were very interested in seeing you. Unfortunately, you were out cold and they couldn't get any answers out of you so they cuffed you to the bed so that you would be here when they returned. Listen, you'll let me know if you need anything won't you?"

"Do you think this is funny? A big joke?"

"No, by no means. I'm just wondering why a man as vicious as yourself wouldn't have attempted to have the corrections made somewhere less obvious."

"What do you mean by vicious. I said I didn't do anything."

"That's not for me to say, but we'll know soon enough. I took the liberty of catheterizing you. I figured since you couldn't get up, you wouldn't want to be bothered with using one hand to hold a bottle to pee in." Letting out a hearty laugh, the doctor left the room. Looking around the room as though searching for a way out, Rich tugged at his restraints to no avail. Finally collapsing to the pillows succumbing to the throbbing pain of his injured hand. He cursed Bob for ever bringing Ivan into her little sexual escapade. Rich could remember clearly Ivan's interview. His demeanor, assured knowing that the position was for him and there was no denying him. Many times Rich warned Bob that her sexual appetite would mark her grave and it did. Even though he helped speed it up a little. Those spineless workers in the past accepted her advances and danced to her music but there was something about Ivan, the moment he saw him that let him know that things would not go as she'd planned.

The more Bob's company grew and her bank book expanded, the greater her desire to control became. Men trembled at her will and bowed to her dollar because she paid them well for their service. Initially, Rich genuinely loved her and worshiped the ground she walked on, guarding and protecting her lascivious appetite, feeding her men who were weak yet capable of satisfying her lustful hunger. Married men, that's what she liked. She enjoyed destroying them, slowly robbing them of what she believed to be power. The greatest force known to mankind love, family and trust. She would buy their love, break up their family and destroy their trust. But not Ivan; He's a man operating at his own will, controlling his own destiny and deciding what his tomorrow will bring. Rich had grown to love watching Barbara aggressively fucking these useless men who wished every moment that she would explode into her twisted ecstacy and release them from their bondage. He would then follow them home to see if after hours of humiliation, that same "love" could be extended to their wives. At first it was easy until finally everything was out in the open and the "bond of love" was broken.

Bob, she never wanted love, she wanted control

and Rich wanted her and would do anything to make her happy, even feeding her men. But he warned her about Ivan and she swore that she would tame him. Ivan was making a pretty hefty salary, a great deal more than other companies would have paid. But what Bob didn't realize is that he was not driven by money but true power - control.

Rich remembered working late that night, the night that Barbara was killed. A new client had called in and needed a contractor quick. He prepared the paperwork and was going to go over it with Bob that night but when he got there, he heard her arguing with Ivan and things weren't going her way. Rich tiptoed upstairs to see what was going on. He could hear Ivan fucking her, his body slapping against hers forcefully, just the way she liked it. Billy and the others never had the balls to do what he was doing for her. Although she couldn't control him, he would be her prize because what he gave her was greater than what she anticipated. She screamed in a way Rich had never heard and he had fucked her many times before. He was her last resort and because of her promised fortune, he could never take her to the limit, never crossing the line. He heard her voice pleading for mercy and Ivan continued to give it to her. Only peeping through a tiny crack in the door Rich watched Ivan's ass bouncing up and down, working in circular motions until Barbara collapsed to the sheets. Not understanding what just happened, Rich hurried downstairs and to his car driving away without turning on his lights. He would come back tomorrow to go over the paperwork. Cursing again, Rich remembered going home and feeling jealous. Of all the times he slept with that woman, never had she given him that kind of performance. Instead, she treated him almost as bad as the others. He was different, he would return to her and show her what he was made of. The clock read ten o'clock p.m. and Rich knew that Ivan would have left by then and home to his wife so he put his clothes on expecting to give her a performance better than Ivan had given earlier.

Unlocking the door to Bob's house, Rich could feel a stillness which was different than anything he had felt before. Everything was silent. Thinking Ivan really wore her out including her entire house. He presumed the walls were tired of the same old fuck routine as well, and it too after receiving a refreshing view, rested, anticipating that another day would bring fresher memories. When he reached the top of the stairs, he heard a light gasping. He hurried into Bob's room finding her lying on the bed face down. She was naked with the stains of semen and shit streaking her ass. Ivan had definitely fucked the shit out of her literally. He wondered why she hadn't changed. That wasn't like her to remain dirty. The thought made Rich angry to think that she relished his talents that much to remain in their lustful filth.

"Bob," he shouted angrily expecting her nonchalant empty stare but she didn't respond. He turned her over to see the trickle of blood escaping her nostril. Her neck carried the tracks of torture revealing the beating she sustained.

"Help me," she managed to say, bleakly looking up into his eyes with a look Rich had never seen before.

"Did Ivan do this to you?" A nod was all she could manage and Rich, disgusted to think that she would allow him to get away with it and so many years she treated him like dirt with only the promise of leaving him her entire fortune to compensate for it. She would never die. She would out live him and all this would have been for nothing. So he did what any man it his right mind would do, take this opportunity to take his gold.

"I'll help you my darling," he promised while pulling her from the bed. Barbara's relief was visual as Richard sat her up in a chair. He placed a pillow in front of her telling her to relax. Her eyes displayed fatigue and weakness and she remained slumped in the chair. Leaning her head back onto the back of the chair, Barbara began to doze off when she received a crashing blow to her chest. Immediately, her eyes opened to find that her angel of mercy was the grim reaper instead. He kicked and kicked at her chest using the pillow as a guard against bruises. Finally when the chair fell back, he continued to stomp with all his might into her sternum until breathing became difficult. Blood trickled from her mouth. Barbara knew that she was going to die and there was nothing anyone could do for her. Finally, the only thing that was left was a wisp of air until her chest collapsed. When he checked for a pulse, there was none to be found. He returned her to the bed where she remained for the guys to find her. Unfortunately, her life remained a few hours too long. Even in death, she would have victory over him. He cursed himself to think that he could be so stupid.

It wasn't long before Rich received a visit from Officers Thompson and Griswold.

"So fella," Thompson teased, "you thought you would get away from us didn't ya?"

"I don't know what you're talking about," he demanded adamantly.

"So tell me why did you do it?"

"Do what?"

"Kill that young girl!"

"What young girl?"

Griswold walking around the bed tapping on the railing with his nightstick. He leaned close to Rich's ear whispering "the one on Twin Pine Drive."

"What do you mean he demanded. I haven't seen her in a couple of weeks. What are you saying? Are you trying to tell me that she's dead?" He continued to petition for answers hoping that what he thought he was hearing wasn't true. "Are you saying that someone killed Geneva?"

"Yes, did you forget killing her too?"

"I didn't kill her. I didn't kill anybody."

"Well, we found pictures of you with her and there's a witness who claims that you used to beat her pretty badly. I've got to tell you that's going to look pretty bad in the eyes of the jury, so I suggest that you just admit it and cop a plea."

"I ain't copping no plea. I didn't kill her and I will not, under any circumstances, take the blame for something that I didn't do."

"Suit yourself. Besides, my job isn't to determine whether you're guilty or not, my job is to bring you in."

"I'm telling you that Ivan is trying to set me up."

"By the way, you wouldn't guess what we found last night."

"What."

"We decided to check out this Ivan character and you wouldn't believe what we found?" Rich waited, refusing to play their little game of charades.

"Someone had broken into Mr. Carty's house and ransacked his bedroom. Who would do a thing like that? Besides, what I found most amusing is that he rigged a little torture device that maimed the person violating his privacy. Since the blood was fresh, I figured, let me check the nearest hospital and see how many people showed up with injuries to the hand.

Guess who we turned up with?" He waited a second and answered himself "you!"

"Wait a minute, I was just looking for some evidence to clear my name. We only hired Ivan a day prior to Bob's death. I warned her that we didn't know enough about him but she insisted on hiring him."

"Didn't he provide you with references?"

"Yes but "

"Then what other information did you require? Isn't that the standard for acquiring a job?"

"Yes, but you don't understand the situation here."

"What situation."

"Barbara liked men."

"So what's so intriguing about that?"

"She hired mainly married workers because she enjoyed taking things that didn't belong to her. Of course when the guys refused, she threatened to fire them and they would continue allowing her to take advantage of them until either she lost the desire for them or their wives left them. Either way, she would always be on the winning end."

"So in other words, you think that when she met Ivan, she bit off more than she could chew?"

"I think that she made a grave mistake messing with him in the first place."

"Why not the other guys. Ivan wasn't the only one working in her home. What makes him so special?"

"Because, don't you see, the others have been working with her for awhile now and if they were going to do something, it would have been done a long time ago."

"Not necessarily, maybe she provided them with an opportunity that wasn't given until now."

"Besides, you're no different, she used to fuck you as well. Maybe you were jealous and decided to kill her."

"I would never hurt Bob or Geneva for that matter. Yes we had our little spats and disagreements and yes there were times when I might have acted out my anger violently but never would I strangle her."

"I never said she was strangled. How would you have known that?"

"I just presumed."

"Lucky guess huh? I don't think so. Listen, let me give you a piece of advice, have your attorney present before you say anything else that might incriminate you."

Fuck! Richard thought constipation of the mind, diarrhea of the tongue. His tongue was still quicker than his brain. Again, he fucked himself without realizing it and what's bad about it is that he really didn't do it.

"So you mean to tell me that because my mouth fouled up again, that the investigation on Ivan is closed? Any suspicions that you might have had at this point no longer exists?"

"Well, the way I see it, it's not my decision to make. You will have to wait to see how my boss feels about it and trust me, he has a thing for you. So no matter what, you're going down for this."

Rich could feel the weight of defeat's cumbersome load pressing against his chest. Certainly he would fry for this one. There was no way he could pin this one on Ivan because he didn't even know him.

"Well," Officer Griswold started "I guess we've covered everything we need to here so we'll be getting back to the station. Thanks for the statement."

"No wait!" Richard shouted. "Doesn't it even peak your curiosity?"

"Does what peak our curiosity?"

"Ivan's reason for needing such a device. Listen, I was looking under his bed and something told me to look between his mattresses and when I had reached between it, I felt something. So I lifted the mattress so that I could take it out when it snapped on my fingers. He would have had to be hiding something to require such a device don't you think?"

"Yeah but we searched everything and we didn't see anything that looked suspicious and perhaps it didn't have anything to do with you. Maybe he didn't want his wife snooping in his belongings and that was his way of keeping her out."

"No, I'm telling you, that was meant for me."

"And why would he be expecting you to be in his house when he's not there. Besides, how did you know that he wouldn't be there?"

"I didn't. I just took a chance. If he had been there, I would have tried to get him to admit to killing her and I would have brought that information to the police."

"Even if he would have admitted it, did you think he would have shared that with us?"

"Of course not, that's why I had a tape recorder."

"Alright, if it will make you feel better, I will see what we can dig up on this Ivan character. But I've got to tell you, I don't see this helping your situation any. Even if we can pin this on Ivan, what about Geneva?"

"I didn't kill her. I don't know what happened to her and I have no idea who would want to hurt her." Thompson jotted that information down on his pad then replaced it in his back pocket, tilted his hat and proceeded out the door followed by Griswold.

Standing in the brisk cold air, Griswold stopped his partner.

"What do you make of this guy?"

"I don't know but perhaps we need to check this

Carty character out. I want to know what this guy was protecting to require such a contraption."

"You've got to admit, that's some crazy shit," he said while chuckling.

"I kind of like the guy. He doesn't say too much and the little he does say is calculated. You can never tell where he's coming from."

"Yeah, I guess you would have to have a true eye to eye with him and hopefully he's not one of those psychopathic killers who doesn't remember or doesn't give a damn. You definitely won't read them."

"So what now? What do you think will happen when he discovers his house has been vandalized?"

"I know what I would do if I came home and found my house broken in to I'd call the police." A hearty laughter followed. They knew that Ivan didn't seem the type to give a perilous call to the locals for help.

"Did you see the size of that guy. There is no way he's going to call us."

"So do we stake out his house?"

"He's clever, he'd spot us a mile away. We would never be able to fool him. I think we should just ask him if he has any idea who would do such a thing."

"Makes sense to me. Lets do it."

Brown walked around to the driver side of the car as Griswold opened the passenger door. He radioed the incident in and headed for the station.

CHAPTER
17

Tammy knew what she had to do the first chance she got; she would go through the employee files and find Nurse Green's home address. Of course with the day being so crazy, she didn't have a chance. First, a guy who comes in during the night with severed fingers is arrested for a murder then she's assigned to his wing. Cops have been in and out all day. The last thing she needed was to be assigned to care for a criminal.

"Alright Mr. Davis, I need to have a look at your dressing and check your vitals. You know the routine stuff. I'm sure by now you're familiar with the routine. The previous shifts have already done it. I'm just repeating procedure."

"Do I detect an attitude nurse?"

"No. Not at all. I just don't want any trouble."

"So, you're already passing judgment huh. For you're information, I'm innocent. There's this guy, Ivan Carty who was hired by my boss, well, was my boss until he killed her, who set me up. All the evidence points to me and now he's killed a girl I was seeing and it seems I'm always right in the middle."

"That's too bad. Either you have a poor choice in women or a bad judgment of character. What ever the problem, seems to me you're already fucked."

"Not if I can get someone to help me."

"Help you do what?"

"Prove that this guy's a killer. Will you help me draw him here?"

"No. I don't want to get involved with any problems you're entangled with. I just want to do my job."

"I see. Well thank you nurse for just doing your job!"

"You're welcome. I'll be back later to check your dressing again. Try not to call me unless it's absolutely necessary."

Hurrying out the room, she rushed back to the nurses' station.

"Stacey can you cover me for a moment? I've got to check on something."

"Sure, I'm not doing anything right now. Hurry back, you know how Nurse Green get's when she can't find staff."

"I'll be gone no longer than ten minutes."

Tammy rushed downstairs to the waiting area and utilized an empty telephone booth. Searching her pockets, she found some change to make a call. After placing a quarter into the phone, she dialed the number on the paper. When ordered, she entered the pin number and waited for the tone. Three beeps followed and she keyed in the numbers found on the telephone followed by the number sign. She hung up the phone when the page was transmitted and awaited the return call. Moments later, she received a response.

"Hello, someone paged me?"

"Hey baby it's me."

"Tammy, you got something for me? You work quickly. I didn't expect to hear from you so soon!"

"No, I didn't get that yet but I have something better for you."

"What's that?"

"There's a patient here who claims that you mur-

dered two people and is trying to frame him. Have any
idea who this person might be?"

"Is it Richard Davis?"

"Bingo! He hurt his hand some time last night and
was put on bed arrest after surgery."

"Surgery? What happened to him?"

"He severed three of his fingers. What ever it was,
it went right through the bone. The guy's lucky he got
here in time, he might have lost them for good."

"That's too bad. So, what are the police saying?
Are they investigating his allegations?"

"I don't think so. He didn't mention any hope. In
fact, he wanted me to help him lure you here. I have
no idea how he intended to do that. I told him I was-
n't interested in helping him seek justice. My job is to
medically take care of him until my shift is over."

"Okay, this is what we're going to do. You don't discuss anything else with him and I'll pay him a visit
later tonight when I think he might be sleeping and
fewer visitors and staff are circling the floors. I'll need
you to give me the word."

"I'll put you in a good place until the time is right.
Listen, I'd better be getting back before I'm missed."

CHAPTER
18

"Good morning my love." Steve loved the way daybreak shone on Angelica's face. If he had his way, he would see the sun rise and set on it for the rest of his life.

"Steve, what happened yesterday? I was so worried about you!"

"Yesterday was just one of those days. Listen, how about we pack our bags and prepare for a nice long vacation?"

"I thought you had surgeries scheduled." He dismissed her concerns. "Honey, there are always surgeries. I'm a surgeon, people rely on me to repair them but I have to repair me sometimes too. Right now, I need time to let my new medication work."

"What medication is that?" she asked smiling at him.

"This one." He said while lifting up the covers exposing his morning rise.

Their giggles faded into the quiet sounds of passion. Steve wished that he could reassure his angel that everything was going to work out but he could see her worry and concern every time he walked into the house. It's as though she half expected to see Ivan or get bad news. No matter how he tried to convince her that Ivan would eventually stop looking, she knew deep inside that Ivan would never truly let her go even if it was the fear he knew he'd left in her memory. No matter what he would always haunt her until he was dead.

When they were comforted by each other's bliss, he continued holding her knowing that although she was at rest, the fear of her husband still remained. He watched her soft grey eyes peering up at him with tiny twinkling tears in them, searching for reassurance.

"Everything will be alright. I'm so sorry you have to go through this, but in the end, it will be well worth it."

He called his travel agent and explained that he wanted a two week getaway for two. After answering a few questions, he hung up the phone. Angelica watched him expecting an itinerary.

"So where to?" She questioned excitedly.

"It's a surprise. Don't worry, you'll like it. My agent plans all of my trips and I've got to tell you, he's the best in his field. He does extensive traveling and know all the memorable spots all over."

"Great! Then perhaps we should go shopping."

"No can do sweetheart. I've got to go to the hospital later to take care of some paperwork. Then you've got me all to yourself for two weeks. Angel, there's something I've been wanting to ask you for some time now and I think now would be the time."

A look of concern came over her face as she half expected the worse. He could see the concern on her face and reassured her that it wasn't that bad. He held her hands, looking into her eyes searching for an answer to the question he hadn't asked.

"Angel, I know this might not be a comfortable time to ask you this but I'm hoping that you will consider being my wife."

The words finally escaped in its tremulous tone. Angelica's shock was apparent. Of all the things she could have been anticipating, marriage was certainly not one of them. How could he ask her to marry him at a time like this? What was she going to do about

Ivan? Although he hadn't mentioned him, she knew that he was still looking for her and probably been to the hospital several times now. In fact, every time the door opens, the first face she sees is Ivan's. She would never get over that fear until he either died or was locked up.

"Steve, what about my husband? You know he'll never let me go?"

"He would have no choice. After the divorce papers are signed, he will have no choice but to let go."

"Is that what you believe? Do you think that's all it takes to get Ivan off my back? He doesn't care about any piece of paper. I am his forever. Until death we do part and he will stand by it totally even if he has to kill me."

"I won't let that happen."

He held her hand a little tighter to reassure her.

"You don't understand, Ivan is not stable. He does not believe in anything being taken from him and he will not for a minute honor that paper. It wouldn't surprise me if he attempted to kill me right in front of the judge."

"Then he would be arrested!"

"He could care less. Everything is important to him. Ivan can't allow anyone to get the best of him. He's very cunning, and just when you think you have him, he turns the table. Darling, it's his way or die."

Steve could feel a chill creep up his spine leaving a slight quiver in the pit of his stomach. It was one thing to be in love with a battered woman but someone attached to a possible killer, that's another. Remembering Ivan at the hospital, he couldn't see him killing anyone. Although he was persistent, he didn't display any traits of psychosis.

"Honey, that's what he wants you to believe. That's

what he wants you to think that there is no way out and no one can help you. Ivan is not invincible."

He could feel his temperament increasing as he tried to convince Angelica that her husband only instilled that fear in her to keep her from leaving him.

"You'll see, Ivan will soon be out of your life and he will never bring any harm to you again. I will protect you even if it cost me my life." Angelica felt sick to think that Ivan might be forced to kill her beloved doctor and there wasn't a doubt in her mind that he would. The one thing she was assured of is that he would and it would be all her fault.

Searching his eyes for reassurance, Angelica felt as though she should cut her loses and return to the dreaded life she once knew. The one that beckoned her return; insisting even without a word. Steve was careful not to mention his altercation with Ivan but the fear that overshadowed her could not be reprieved. It was like a dark eclipse had come into her life forever blocking her from seeing any other way of living. She would never be loved and certainly not by anyone who knew the true meaning.

"Steve, I'm afraid. I love you, very, very much and there is nothing other than this that would keep me from saying yes but you've got to understand that the moment we have to sit in front of an attorney or judge I will be face to face with the one who has tormented and controlled me since I left my parents on our North Carolina farm. I don't want to be responsible for you getting hurt. It was a good idea but I think that you should consider what you're asking me to do. You're asking me to go against Satan himself. Yes, I know eventually he would be eradicated but until then, I will have to live in fear. Do you know what that's like?"

"No, but I fear for you and what my life would be

like without you! Of course I know this is no where near what you're feeling but certainly I share that same feeling. Honey things will work out. You'll see. If none of this happened, would you have married me?"

"Without a second thought."

"Then let's pretend that Ivan never existed and you and I met at some coffee shop and started talking over a donut and after some time of seeing each other you realized that you loved me as much as I have you and I asked you to marry me."

He picked up her hand and looked into her eyes trying to get her to be captured into the zone. "Marry me my Angel Oh, I know what's wrong! Wait a minute."

He got up from the bed and walked over to the closet and reached into the inside pocket of his suit jacket and pulled out a little box. Returning to the bed, he knelt down on one knee, held her left hand focusing on her pretty grey eyes. He opened the little black box exposing a two-carat-princess cut diamond with baguettet diamonds along the side, set in pure platinum.

"Angelica, my sweet Angelica will you marry me and allow me to help you forget all that's ever troubled you and caused you hurt and harm and made you unhappy? Let me show you, as my wife, what life should be like?" He waited for a response hoping she didn't forget the scenario he set for her.

"Yes, Dr. Steven Painkin, I will marry you under the conditions you previously described."

"You know that almost sounded like a genuine acceptance."

"It was! I love you even enough to die."

He placed the ring on her finger and held her close to him.

"You won't die. Ivan will never hurt you again."

CHAPTER

19

"Tammy on her break went to the employee files where she searched for Nurse Green's phone number and address. It was seven o'clock p.m. and everyone had left already. She placed gum between the lock earlier so that the door wouldn't lock. After going through several cabinets, she located it. She wrote down the address then searched for Dr. Painkin's.

"Excuse me, what are you doing in here. This is a restricted area. What were you doing?"

"Oh, I was looking for a file on one of the patients." She responded to the woman who startled her.

"Not in here you weren't. Seems to me you've lost your way. Maybe I need to report you to administration."

Tammy could feel the anger building up. Finding her in the file room was definitely questionable but not to the extreme with which she was taking it.

"Listen, as I said before, I just lost my way and it won't happen again. I'm certain that I have caused no harm here."

"This is a very sensitive area. This is the only protection we can offer for our employees. If anyone can just walk in here and access files, what protection are we really offering them?"

"I can appreciate where you're coming from but as I said before, I didn't mean to cross any lines. I simply wanted to find a record on a patient and didn't realize that I was in the wrong place. I'm new here and haven't really learned my way around yet. Certainly you can understand that. Would it really make sense to report me to my superiors causing a big fuss over nothing which may in turn cause me to lose my job over something as minute as this? I know you can't be that cold!"

She gave a pleading smile, but deep down, she would kill her if she had to. The nurse shrugged and decided that perhaps she was right, this was too petty to report.

"Okay, this time I will let it slip but I had better not catch you in here again."

"You don't have to worry about that. I certainly know now that this is not the patient file room and definitely not the place for me. Thanks for understanding." For once she thought to herself that she would do something kind for someone else without expecting something in return. In fact, it felt good. "Listen, just get out of here before I change my mind."

Tammy hurried out and back to the elevators. In the meantime, the nurse went to the file cabinet with which she saw Tammy searching attempting to locate any file of interest. Everyone listed were basically nurses, none of which should be of personal interest. After having found nothing to be concerned about, she felt a slight consolation in knowing that no harm could be done. Too many people die because of carelessness and oversights. By the time Tammy had returned to her floor, everyone were whispering about the murder of Carol Baker. Showing genuine concern, Tammy questioned the means of murder, and one of the nurses responded.

"From what I hear her neck was broken."

"Was she rapped? Robbed?"

"No, that's the funny thing about it. There was no

indication of foul play. Her purse was still in the car
with probably all of its original contents, there was at
least two hundred dollars cash with a withdrawal
receipt indicating that money was taken yesterday
afternoon. Also two money orders, one for seventy-
eight dollars and the other for nine hundred fifty dollars, which had not been filled out yet. I assume she
was going to pay a bill."

"No, she was sending money to her daughter who's
away in college. Her daughter needed furniture for her
room so she was sending it to her."

"Why didn't the guy take the money?"

"You're assuming it was a guy who did it."

"Of course. What woman do you know walking
around who could break someone's neck?"

"You never know. So do they have any ideas?"

"Not from what I can tell. There's no evidence.
Perhaps she put up too much of a fight and he had to
kill her before doing anything and felt that his ploy had
been compromised."

"Hmm, I can see where you're coming from."

"Does Green know about it?"

"Yeah, she's in her office now rearranging sched-
ules."

Nurse Green dialed Dr. Painkin's number. The
phone rang only once when an unfamiliar voice
answered. She knew that it could only have been
Angelica.

"Mrs. Carty, is that you?"

"Who's speaking please?"

"This is Nurse Green from the hospital. Is Steve
there? It's really important that I speak with him."

"Is everything all right?"

"Oh yeah, yeah, I just wanted to give him some
news about one of our employees. Nothing to be

alarmed about."

"Well, he had to step out for a while, he'll be back later on tonight."

"Tell him that I'm on my way home now and that he should call me there. I really need to speak to him before you two go away."

"Are you sure that there isn't a problem? Does this have anything to do with me or my husband?"

"No, he was just really close with one of the nurses here and I wanted to let him know that she had died."

"Oh. I'm sorry to hear that. I'll make sure to tell him the moment he returns."

"Good. You take care of yourself."

Her statement struck Angelica funny. She sounded pretty anxious for someone who just wanted to inform someone of a death of an employee. She wondered if it had anything to do with Ivan. Wondering if he was still searching for her. Well actually, the question wasn't if he was still looking for her but to what lengths. Would he actually kill the hospital staff to find her? She imagined that this whole situation must have him feeling pretty unstable especially since it wasn't in his nature to let anything get away from him. He would die before he would allow anyone or anything to come between them. She stood at the window, as usual expecting to find him lurking between the shadowy dimness cast by the mass of trees outside surrounding the house. Sometimes even the fountain statue gave way to insecurity.

Nurse Green looked over the charts again making certain that everything was in order and everyone knew what needed to be done. Looking at her watch, she realized that she had better be going. Her younger sister was coming over for the weekend and she wanted to start making preparations for her arrival. Grabbing her trench from her cubby, she remembered that she had promised a patient that she would bring him medicine for pain. At first, she thought to instruct Tammy to take care of it but sometimes promises are more important than just getting the job done. She looked into his room and he was fast asleep. She shook him to awake him.

"Mr. Davis, here are the painkillers I promised you. You had better wake up now, you can't do it for yourself."

He didn't respond. She noticed that his bandages were severely soaked with blood and needed attention right away. She imagined that he was trying to squeeze his hands from the cuffs and injured his already damaged hand. Twenty-four hours hadn't even passed since his surgery and already he was trying to escape.

"Poor fellow," she thought presuming that he passed out from the pain. She shook him again trying to get a response when something told her to check his vitals. Placing her fingers at his wrist, then his throat, she realized that he had no pulse. Immediately, she rushed out into the corridor screaming for assistance, half knowing that it was too late. Her patient had died right under her nose after having no record of sickness or terminal injury. "What the fuck is going on here?"

"What's wrong?"

"Who last saw this patient. I want to know what happened to this guy who was perfectly healthy no more than an hour ago. He was just relaxing waiting for the officers to return and harassing me for painkillers. I promised him that I would return shortly and I got tied up with the Carol incident. Now this!"

Silve, one of the circulating nurses pulled Nurse Green to the side and began whispering...

"I don't know if this has anything to do with this

but he was telling me that someone by the name of
Ivan Carty was trying to frame him for the murder of
his boss and also his girlfriend. He also said that he
was responsible for what had happened to his hand.
He said that if I didn't help him get out of here that he
would be in great danger. He believes that this Ivan
character would eventually find out where he was and
would try to kill him since he had confronted him the
other day."

The name itself brought chills to Nurse Green. She
began to tremble uncontrollably.

"Nurse Green, do you know this guy?"

"No, no, it's just that this happened right before our
eyes and no one noticed him. How could that be? Did
you see anyone come in to visit him?"

"No. About thirty minutes ago, I thought I heard
someone yell but it was so faint that I couldn't locate it.
I checked the rooms and everything seemed to be all
right. In fact, Mr. Davis seemed to be sound asleep."

Nurse Green couldn't wait another minute. She
hurried out the door without following normal proce-
dures. She needed to notify Steve that Ivan was after
him. Then she remembered that Carol was the one
who signed out his wife the night she left the hospital.
That explains why she was killed. He probably followed her and killed her before she could seek the
refuge of her home.

"Dammit, why didn't I pay attention? This is your
fault Steve. I told you that this was not a good idea.
Your coveting is costing too many lives."

She raced to her car looking behind and to her
sides, hoping not to run into Ivan. Finally, she could
see her car and the struggled to remove her keys so
that she wouldn't be delayed when she got there when
someone grabbed her from behind...

"Nurse Green, are you okay?"

"Oh, yes Phil, I just wanted to get home as quickly as possible. I have company coming over and I want to get there before they got there. I was supposed to do some things but I didn't have the chance so now I'm rushing to get it done."

He turned to walk away, wondering how something so trivial could get a stiff neck like her to hustle.

"Hey, how about escorting me to my car?"

"Sure why not. You're not making a pass at me are you?"

He expected to see her usual dry look but she had a look of desperation. It was a look of fear and expectation, one that he knew so well in women.

"Are you expecting something to happen? Is someone after you Nurse Green?"

"No, what would make you say that? Listen I think I can make it from here. My car is just over there. I can see it now."

He knew something was wrong but he could also tell that it was something that she didn't want to talk about. He could read women very well and whatever or who ever it is, she's got her nose stuck right in the middle of the shit and don't want anyone to know about it. Why else would she protect someone who's stalking her?

"I think I feel more comfortable escorting you to your vehicle. I would hate to hear that a pretty woman like yourself was hurt during my shift, especially when I could have at the very least helped you to your car."

"Thanks. I appreciate that."

She was quiet the entire walk to the car and he knew that she was grateful more so than she tried to show.

"Okay, this is my car. I'll be fine now. Thanks

again for chaperoning me."

"Anytime." He waited for her to remove her club and start her car. When she was safely leaving the parking lot, he returned to his post at the hospital doors.

Rushing to her house, she wondered if Steve had returned and if Angelica remembered to give him the message. She hoped that when he received the message that he would know that the code was to call immediately or stop by.

≈≈

The moment Steve walked into the house; he could see that there was something going on.

"Angel, is there something wrong?"

"No, I guess not. Nurse Green asked me to tell you to call her at home right away that one of the employees died, someone you were very close to."

"Who was it?"

"She didn't say but from the tone in her voice, I know that it must have been more to it than what she tried to display. She seemed pretty anxious, not like her calm self."

Steve rushed to the phone and dialed her number at home. Waiting no answer. Not even her machine picked up. He waited until her phone had rung about twenty times or at least long enough that when he had hung up the phone, he could still hear the ringing in his ears. He called the hospital to see if anyone else got the news. When he called the hospital, Silve answered at the station.

"Hello Dr. Painkin, what can I do for you? Are you about ready for your trip?"

"Yeah sure, but I need to speak to Nurse Green right away."

"Sorry, she left already. You won't believe it but

Carol is dead. Someone murdered her and worse than that, there was a patient here under hospital arrest and he was trying to tell me that someone was after him and trying to kill him and within thirty minutes, he was murdered too. I don't know what's going on but I'm ready to get out of here.

Tammy already left, but her shift was over anyway. I told Nurse Green the patient said that someone named Ivan Carty was after him, she seemed a little concerned."

"Thanks Silve, I'll try to reach her at home. You had better get on the phone and give that information to the officers that are handling the case. Let me know what happens."

He hung up the phone and hurried out the door yelling back at the house.

"Angel, I'll be back shortly, I'm going over to see Nurse Green. Don't let anyone in and I'll call you on my way back."

"Honey, what's going on? I don't like being kept in the dark. Is my husband after her. You've got to "

Before she could finish her sentence, he was in the car and already pulling out the driveway. There was a pulling at the pit of her stomach. Steve, Nurse Green and the entire hospital, any and everyone who stood in Ivan's way in pursuit of his wife would be killed. Angelica knew this and everyone's actions let her know that it wouldn't be long now before he got to her or died trying.

✍۶

Nurse Green had made it safely to her home and everything seemed to be in order. She kicked off her shoes and went to her phone to call Steve. There was certainly no time to lose and every moment counted. She checked her answering machine to see if any calls were left. The funny thing was there was no status showing. Even if there were no messages, it would still display the zero. She checked the plug and it was fine. She picked up the receiver expecting that there would be no dial tone but there was. She dialed Angelica to see if Dr. Painkin had arrived.

"Hello Angelica, did he return yet?"

"Yeah, but he's on his way to your place. He really seemed concerned. I wish that one of you would tell me what's going on."

"Mrs. Carty, there's nothing to worry about."

Just then, the phone cut off and standing at the kitchen door no more than five feet away was the one she feared the most. His deep penetrating eyes stabbed at her as she observed him leaning against the entrance of the kitchen. Nurse Green could feel the fear building within her, compelled to answer and yet resisting the temptation. Knowing that inevitably she would die. Denying the obvious would only increase his fury and add to the punishment she realized was coming. Realizing there was no need to run, she awaited what was to come. He casually walked over to her and gestured for her to have a seat. Obliging him, she sat on the sofa, which was right next to her.

"Tssk, tssk, tssk. I guess you thought you had me fooled didn't ya? Do you know that after being with a woman for so many years you would certainly know their limitations? Had you said to me that she was questioned by the police and was offered some sort of protective custody I would have been more receptive and assumed the truth was being told but as we know, that wasn't the case. You said she signed herself out without calling anyone or being picked up by anyone. Now Angelica wouldn't do something like that, especially on her own. She does what she's told, she's a humble woman, eager to please and certainly not a leader, so there was no way she would have left me without being literally ordered to do so. And my instinct told me that it was the good old doctor, who had from the moment he laid eyes on her, took personal umbrage to her. Very unprofessional I might add. So since time is of essence, I need only one thing from you and I hope that you will make this as easy as possible and I will make it as painless as possible. You know that you deserve all that's coming to you and I'm already disappointed in your lying before. So, how are we going to do this? Will it be easy or will I have to do the torture thing?"

"What do you want?"

Smiling with his handsome features, he indicated that he was glad she made that choice.

"Where can I find my wife? And don't tell me you don't know because you were just speaking with her. I could have killed you before you got here if I wanted to. But I decided that I would give you a chance to make up for some of your wrong doings. Did you know that God says that what he has yoked together let no man put asunder? You should not have aided in taking her away. So where is she?"

He questioned, leaning close to her after taking a seat next to her on the sofa. Teasing her intimately as he loved to do, of course meaning nothing by it, but it did what he wanted it to and that was to make her feel uncomfortable.

"She's at Dr. Painkin's home."

"Very good. You deserve a G.I. Joe badge for that. How about telling me something I don't know like where he lives."

He got up and walked behind the couch and began massaging her shoulders. He could tell she was tense and frightened of him and what he was going to do.

She quickly began reciting the information he requested hoping that he would realize that she was truthful about the information and not torture her as he'd promised. Ivan recorded the information by repeating it and waited for her confirmation. The first time, he recited the address incorrectly wanting to see if she would correct him. When she did, he quickly snapped her neck. Her eyes stared up at him. Even in death, her troubled look remained. He tilted his head while observing her, wondering whether or not he should close her eyes. Nah he thought, no need spoiling the art. It's not easy capturing a person's emotions in death. Peace would not be found in her face because now that she's answered to him, she would have to answer to the almighty for her sins against the vows he and Angelica had taken.

Heading for the door, he said aloud "Now for you Dr. Painkin." He didn't think to lock the door, he left it slightly ajar focusing on finally seeing Angelica again. It had been a long time since he had seen her. Although he realized that he would have to kill her, he would make love to her one last time and Dr. Painkin would witness it for himself through the cold stare of death. Returning to his vehicle, he drove to the nearest pay phone and called the transportation hotline. He requested direction for the address he was given. After receiving it, he hung up the phone.

CHAPTER

20

Angelica heard the doorbell ringing and she remembered what Dr. Painkin had told her. She was not to answer the door, but she was tired of hiding and if it was indeed Ivan, she would tell him herself to leave her alone and that she no longer wanted to be with him. Of course she knew that he wouldn't go away quietly and certainly, if nothing else, go into his usual rage and try to kill her. Only difference, he wouldn't expect her to fight back.

She went into the study and found in Dr. Painkin's bag a scalpel, the sharpest knife known to man. She would perform surgery on him and cut out the damaged parts, the ones that made him so detestable his hands, his feet, his heart. He didn't deserve to live and Angelica realized that killing was a sin but it was better him than her. The doorbell jolted her out of her sinister thought. She returned downstairs and peered through the side panel. It was a nurse from the hospital. She was probably looking for Steve. Thinking for a moment, she wondered if she should let her in or tell her that he wasn't at home.

"Angelica Carty? Hi my name's Tammy. I'm one of the nurses from St. Agnes Hospital. Dr. Painkin told me to come by and keep you company until he arrived. He told me that he would be away longer than he'd anticipated and didn't want you to be alone for so long."

Angelica felt a slight relief. She told her just a minute and felt silly holding such a sharp object in her hand. Besides, she didn't want the young lady to think that she was paranoid. She probably doesn't know why she's here and the kind of danger she's in. She hurried into the kitchen and placed the scalpel in the utensil draw along with the butter knives. Then she returned to the door and opened it.

The woman was young and beautiful, the type that Ivan would love to get his hands on. She looked innocent, sheepish and naive.

"So, when did you speak to Dr. Painkin? Is he okay?"

"Sure, sure, he wanted to make certain that you were okay. A lot has happened at the hospital today. One of the patients under his care just died and he wanted to see what had happened. I'm sure that Nurse Green mentioned that to him and that's why he wanted me to come here, just in case it took longer than he'd anticipated." She noticed that there were suitcases packed and placed at the door.

"Were you two going somewhere?"

"Yeah, Steve felt that we needed a vacation. In fact, we're leaving tomorrow morning."

"Oh that sounds great, where are you going?"

"I don't know. I don't even care, just as long as it's away from here."

"I hear you girl, everyone needs a break sometime from the monotony of everyday living."

"You can say that again. Can I get you anything while we wait?"

"Nah, I just think that I'll sit here and relax with you. Anything on your mind that you'd like to get off? You seem to be troubled about something."

Angelica noticed that she had been fidgeting since

she came in and wondered what she had to be nervous about. Her expression was changing by the minute, it was as though anger from deep within was building and she wasn't going to be able to keep it bottled up much longer.

"Tammy I was just wondering if you noticed whether or not Dr. Painkin had any bags with him when he arrived because he promised that he would do some shopping before he returned and I want to make certain that he had taken care of it?"

The question took Tammy by surprise, snapping her out of her obvious trance.

"Oh yeah, he did have some bags in his hands. He put them in his office. It looked like clothing."

Angelica knew instantly that she had not talked to him and that he didn't send her so her next question was what did she want with her? Trying to remain calm, Angelica asked Tammy if she could get her anything while she went to get something to drink.

"No thanks, I'm fine."

Angelica got up and began walking to the kitchen when she's struck from behind.

"What are you doing?"

"You stupid bitch! You mean to tell me that you don't recognize trouble when you see it? I'm here to kill you!"

"Why? I don't even know you. What have I done to upset you?"

"Ivan sent me, he wanted me to take care of you, so here I am."

Again, she struck her with her hands clasped together. Angelica tried to fight back but the first blow still had her a little fuzzy. When she had gotten control of the situation, Tammy sprayed mace in Angelica's eyes, rendering her temporarily blind. She straddled over her and removed a scalpel from her purse.

"Stop struggling and make this easy for me. I'm going to give Ivan your heart. If you keep still this can be over with in a moment."

Angelica's pleas were unanswered. She wondered why Ivan would send someone else to kill her. It just didn't sound like something he would do. Tammy began using the scalpel to cut the buttons on Angelica's sweater away, then her bra letting her breasts fall apart.

"I don't see what Ivan saw in you because your breasts are certainly too large to be appreciated."

Now everything made sense. This woman wanted Ivan to herself and she knew that the only way she could have him would be to get rid of her.

"Do you know what would happen if Ivan found out that you did this?" Angelica began, taunting Tammy.

"Yeah, he would thank me. Do you think that you are so precious to him that he would just stop living without you?"

Angelica laughed while fighting the pain in her eyes. Her chest felt as though it would cave in as the weight of Tammy's body became more cumbersome as the minutes passed. She could feel the cold blade resting on her torso. The sharp tip pricked her just below her rib cage when she had taken a deep breath. She guessed that Tammy wanted to torment her first before killing her.

"You know Ivan may have told you that he was going to kill me and I can guarantee you that if he finds me, he will, but he will definitely kill you if you do it for him."

"You've got to be kidding me. You really believe that this man cares that much about you. I guess you know by now that I fucked him. And he taste good too.

I know you must miss that because Dr. Painkin certainly doesn't have anything on him. I don't know what
would have possessed you to choose him to runaway
with but I think you made a grave mistake. Ivan and I
are going to be together after this."

"Really? Well, I give you my blessings. I've got to
tell you that after living with Ivan for five years and getting beat whenever something went wrong, you don't
need to kill me for me to let go. That's why I'm here. I
don't want him anymore. So you can go away and tell
him that you took care of me and I can assure you that
I will never attempt to come between the two of you."

Her statement only angered Tammy. How dare she
try to taint his reputation and degrade his importance?
The man had given her everything. She raised her
hand preparing to plunge the knife into her when the
door came crashing in. Tammy was so busy arguing
with Angelica that she hadn't heard him break the
glass panel and unlock the door. He rushed over to her
planting his foot deep into her back causing her to go
sailing across the floor. He hurried over to her and
began beating her mercilessly, telling her that she had
crossed the line.

"No one gets away with hurting my Angel, not even
you."

"Ivan, I thought you wanted me. You said that once
Angelica was taken care of that you and I would be
together. I was just trying to help you."

"That's the problem, you were doing something I
didn't ask you to do. He looked over to where Angelica
laid, making certain that she was unhurt ,with his
hands still squeezing the life from Tammy's neck. He
resented having to kill her, especially since she had
done so much for him. If it wasn't for her getting a bed
in the same room as Richard, he would never have

been able to get his hands on him without getting caught. When Richard had closed his eyes to relax, Ivan made his move. He pulled the curtain around blocking the view of anyone passing by and held a pillow over his face until the life left him. He was surprised that he still didn't get caught since he made so much noise with his handcuffs. He fought hard to stop Ivan but his restraints held him in place. Ivan squeezed his hand to let him feel a little pain before he left. And of course it helped his suffering end much sooner since he released what little oxygen he still had in him. When the body between his hands ceased to move, he kissed her one last time and dropped her to the floor.

Angelica still blinded by the mace continued to fight to clear her eyes. Ivan could tell that there was something wrong with her eyes and that she couldn't see him. He had missed her so much. "Angel, you look good. I can see that Dr. Painkin has taken good care of you."

He expected to receive a response but received none. She didn't even plead for mercy as she usually did. Then again, he thought, what's the use, she knew that he was going to kill her. He had to kill her, after all she had put him through. "Honey do you know how many people had to die so that I could once again be rejoined with the woman I married?" No response. "You didn't give me a chance to tell you how sorry I was and that I had gotten a new job, of course my new boss tried to take advantage of me but, let me assure you, she received her just reward. No, I didn't kill her, my supervisor did. Why? Because he wanted her money since he couldn't have the woman. The thing about it was that she had left it all to him anyway. All he had to do was wait another thirty or so years until she

died." Ivan had to laugh at that. "Of course, if Rich
was half the man he was he would have gotten it anyway. Anyhow, she's no longer with us and neither is
Rich. Oh, Rich was seeing this pretty young thing at
the Seven Eleven that seemed to have the hots for me
too. Things didn't work out in her favor either.
Besides, you can't blame me; at least I gave her a way
out. All she had to do was leave me alone. Her per-
sistency killed her. I told her I was married and you
know what?" Pausing for a moment as though he
expected a response

"She wanted me anyway. So of course I gave it to
her. You know I could never be selfish. I mean, she
deserved something for sacrificing herself for the
cause. I know, I forgot to tell you the cause....framing
Rich again. Oh, I forgot to mention, I killed him today.
I killed Ms. Seven Eleven a few weeks ago. When I saw
his picture in her apartment, I knew that this would be
the perfect alibi. There would be no doubt that he
killed Bob. Oh, that's my boss. Honey there's just so
much I have to tell you and the sad thing is that I don't
have a lot of time to give you all the details, but being
the kind guy that I am, I'm not going to leave a sole out.
You will know about everybody who died while you
were away."

Angelica felt sick. Did he really think she wanted
to hear this? Or was this his way of tormenting her.

"You remember Carol, the nurse that signed you
out the night you decided to go eloping with the doctor?
Well, I killed her too. Didn't fuck her though. Can you
believe she didn't want me? Of course, I knew she was
only pretending and that was fear speaking. She probably thought I was going to hurt her. I wouldn't have
you know. I would have given it to her the way she
wanted it. I've got sense enough to know that every

woman doesn't like it rough. But you do don't cha darling. You probably didn't think I knew about that little hot note you had in you. In fact, it wouldn't surprise me if you weren't the one who flirted with the old doctor, who is probably on his way here right now. Oh Angel, I wish that things could go back to the way they were. Why did you make me have to kill you? Huh, didn't I take care of you? I know the last time I took things a little too far but I tried to help you and how did you repay me? By running away with the doctor. He can't be fulfilling to you. What did he do, show you his sensitive side?" He said with a note of sarcasm.

"Anyway, I met Tammy here and yes, I've got to admit it that we were going to be one. Or at least in the since of being together, but of course you've got to know that I would never have allowed her to hurt you. You see what happens when women start running crazy? Try to do things that don't make sense. Now she didn't think that I was man enough to handle my own business, so she had to die. I've got to give her some credit, she helped me find Nurse Green, who is dead now. I took care of her tonight and I'm sure that momentarily I will take care of the source of our little problem too. Nurse Green was kind enough to give me your new address so here I am. Enough about me, what have you been up to? I can see that you've been well taken care of. Living out here amongst the rich. Is that what attracted you to him?"

He lifted her holding her so close to him that she could feel the oxygen escaping her lungs. She wondered how long it would take for him to kill her. Would he squeeze her to death or beat her as usual? In her mind, she knew that death was eminent and she would not give him the benefit of her cries. She would accept whatever he had to offer and hope that he would leave her Steve alone.

There was a sound outside. Angelica listened closely to determine what it was. Ivan left the door wide
open when he entered. Certainly Steve would know
that there must be a problem. Then car lights shone
through the windows casting its radiance on the walls.
Ivan turned to look when two officers entered the house
with their guns already pulled.

"Mr. Carty step away from the woman with you
hands out in front of you where I can see them, and
please don't make me repeat myself, its been a long day
and I won't hesitate to shoot you!"

His voice was stern and direct. The other officer
watched purposefully, never lowering his gun nor
relaxing his finger. And by the looks of him, he enjoyed
the potential of inflicting pain. Ivan without reluctance
released Angelica and backed away, holding his hands
out at either side. He was then instructed to lay flat on
the floor and await further instructions. He did as
directed and no punishment was required, which did-
n't seem to go well with the latter officer. He seemed to
be looking forward to a rumble.

"Ma'am are you okay? My name is Thompson and
this is Griswold. We were informed by the hospital that
your husband was responsible for the murder of a
patient in our custody. Nurse Green told us that he
would probably be looking for you here and that we
should hurry up and get here."

Their focus returned to Ivan. You've been a very
busy man Mr. Carty. You're in the line of work that
keep guys like us busy. We like that. Handcuffs were
placed around his wrists and he was then lifted from
the floor.

"Mrs. Carty, do you require any medical attention?"
noticing the bloodstain on her sweater. A van from the

coroner's office arrived. After confirming the death, the body was removed.

"No, I'll be just fine. I'm glad you got here when you did. Have you heard or seen Dr. Painkin?"

"No, but I imagine that he'll be along soon. Well, we're going to be getting this guy down to the station. We'll need you to come down soon for questioning."

"That will be fine. By the way, someone should check on Nurse Green, Ivan had mentioned that she was murdered as well. I'm sorry that I don't know where she lives but I'm sure if you call the hospital, someone can get that information for you."

"We'll do ma'am. Now you take care. Here's my card if you need anything"

She took the card from his hand and looked at it.

"Okay let's go." Griswald said directing Ivan to exit the house. He held Ivan by the arm escorting him out. Surprisingly, Ivan didn't put up a fight. He left peacefully only leaving a cold stare behind. He kept his hands clasped together behind him as though he had done nothing wrong. Angelica stood at the door relieved that everything was over and she could finally go on with her life. She watched the unmarked car pull out of the driveway and onto the street. Finally disappearing as it got further away from the house. She closed the door and locked it. Then she laughed to herself wondering why she bothered locking it. She went upstairs and sat on the bed. She looked at the clock wondering why Steve hadn't arrived yet. He must have gotten stuck in traffic or something or maybe when he got to Nurse Green's house she wasn't dead and was there trying to help her. Then she remembered that she could dial *69 and call back the last incoming call. The phone only rung. After a while, she hung up.

The door swung open rapidly, strking the wall.

From the corner of her eye, she saw a shadow figure rushing over to her. She sat up in fear prepared to fight.

"Angel, you're all right! I am so sorry I left you. I've been trying to get here and it seemed like everything wanted to go wrong. Honey I was afraid that you were hurt or that he had taken you away from me."

"No, I'm fine, the police arrived in time. Nurse Green told the police to come here. Steve Ivan has been arrested."

"Well, Honey, that's good news. We can go on with our lives now."

"Steve he didn't even put up a fight."

"I'm just glad you're okay. I saw the coroner's van. If the police took Ivan, who's body did they claim?"

"Nurse Tammy."

"What was Tammy doing here?"

"She was apparently having an affair with my husband and became obsessed with him. She was trying to kill me and Ivan stopped her permanently."

"Then he had no intentions of killing you, he wanted things to return to the way they were?"

"No, he was going to kill me, he just didn't want anyone else to do it. He believes that no matter what, he must protect me from any and everyone. Our issues as man and wife have nothing to do with anything else. He was going to finish what he came here to do, the police just beat him to the punch."

"Well I'm glad they got here because I don't know what I would have done if I had lost you." He held her close to him absorbing the relief of knowing that this terror was finally over.

❧

It was a long drive to the precinct and Ivan didn't think the trees would ever end. It reminded him of the little town with which he met his wife where people lived so far from each other and there was nothing to see for miles besides vegetation and livestock. Of course, there was no livestock or vegetation but it certainly had the same resemblance.

Griswold sat at the right hand side of Ivan exchanging crime stories with his partner while Ivan listened in amusement slowly working his way out of his cuffs. While being prostrated on the floor, he grasped a paper clip and slid it up his sleeve. While walking to the car he had just enough time to loosen them. He remembered when he was young and his father used to play cops and robbers with him and he had taught him how to find the release lever inside the cuffs. Hours would pass before he would be able to free himself and his father would spank him for taking so long. He said, "son let nothing conquer you neither woman, beast nor object and always keep your guard up." Through tough discipline and punishment, he learned the trick behind unlaching the cuff trick. Now it would take him no more than two minutes to do it. He laughed to himself, because his cuffs were already loose when he was put into the car. Finally he pulled his hands from the cuffs and turned to face the officer sitting next to him.

"What are you looking at?" he questioned threatening to render him some behavioral lessons when Ivan stabbed him in the eye with the paper clip. He squealed trying to stop the bleeding and pain. Thompson looked up in the rearview about to question his partner when Ivan pulled Griswold's gun from his left ankle and fired a shot to the back of his head. The car ran uncontrollably off the road and into a row of bushes which brought the car to a stop. Griswold caught it close range in the face splattering his blood all over the front windshield and seats. It was a pure mess, the windows glistened in crimson blood. Ivan removed the other cuff from his wrist and threw them to the floor. He looked at his watch, cursing, too much time had elapsed.

Anyhow, Dr. Painkin should be home by now and he would give him the surprise he deserve. Opening the door, Ivan pushed Griswold out the door and onto the ground. Then he walked around the car and opened Thompson's door. He fell to the floor the moment the door was opened. Ivan used the newspaper in the passenger's seat to cover the seat then he got in. He backed the car out of the bushes and back onto the road. He made a U-turn and headed for Dr. Painkin's house. These two knucklehead cops just cost him time. Something he didn't have a great deal of. Ivan stopped the car just a quarter mile away.

Ivan watched Dr. Painkin comfort his wife through the window, cloaking her in the comforts of his arms, and he, remorseless for the crimes he committed.

"Three members of his staff were murdered because of his lack of professionalism. They must have been like pawns in a chess game. You have to give a little to gain a lot. What did he think he could do for her? He can't even protect her. Where was he when she needed him the most? Two simple cops came to her rescue. Is that all they thought it would take to bring me down?" Ivan said.

The thought angered him more to think they didn't give him the credit he deserved. Painkin would pay for the damage he caused. He had taken Angelica from him permanently and there was no way he would ever get away with that. It was his fault that he would have to kill her. Kill her, he ingested again as it brought a bitter taste to his mouth. He regretted having to do that but it was the only way to make it right.

He continued sitting there waiting for the right time to drop in and pay the happy couple a visit. Leaning back against the car seat, he checked the gun borrowed from Officer Griswold noticing that he had more than enough for the job. Of course, he didn't want to shoot him, he wanted to cut out that stupid part that made him think that he could get away with what he'd done.

෧ඌ

Meanwhile, Steve prepared a nice soothing bath for his Angel with candles lit all around the oversized tub. He brushed her hair back from her face revealing her lovely eyes. There was great pain and anxiety in them. He tried to tell her that it was all over but she didn't want to believe him. She knew Ivan and there was no way that these guys would be able to stop him from finishing what he came here to do. She expected him to walk in any moment and reclaim the life he sought to eliminate.

Steve leaned down to kiss her forehead...

"Honey, why do you insist on allowing him to control you? It's over now. Didn't you say he was arrested? He will not be able to harm you anymore. He killed too many people to ever be released. I'm sure they will guard him with the caution deserved."

His words were like running water, because she knew that this was not the end and just as the seconds raced by, so was her time. After washing her from head to toe, Steve carried her to the bedroom and massaged her with oils containing peppermint extract to relieve tension. Finally, she relaxed. Maybe this was the beginning of her new life and she just wasn't receptive of it. Steve sensed her sexuality ripening. He could always tell when she wanted him because there was a certain movement she had when he touched her.

Sucking her big toe, then the rest, a sigh of pleasure escaped her lips. He continued across to the other foot, then up her legs slowly resting at the curve of her leg behind her knee. Flinching at his gentle touch, Angelica grasped her pillow trying not to allow the laughter to escape as he tickled her thighs by seductively bitting them. He continued up, burying his face in her ass, tasting it, loving it, caressing and massaging the round fluffiness on the outside. Rolling it in the palms of his hands. She had a great ass, when she laid down, it continued to stand firmly at attention. You could climb on it, bounce on it, roll on it and it still continued to stand. Grabbing her waist, he lifted her up creating a cave between her body and the sheets. Laying on his back, he slid under her as though checking the brakes, orally manipulating her into submission. She began a rhythm of her own pressing her furry mound onto his face.

"Oh shit," he thought, "she's caving in on me." Working his tongue faster he made her cry out her love for him. That feeling she longed for neared. It was so close she could taste it. He knew it too because she trembled with expectation. He welcomed the downpour she was about to release as she continued to work her body. She was now in a squatting position, giving herself more leverage and attempting for force her flow down. Steve watched her breasts bouncing vigorously above him wondering if they would fall on him like coconuts off a tree. Steve stroked his organ preparing to give her just the relief she liked after being eaten.

"Aaaaah", she yelled. Steve had never known her to have an orgasm like this one. She jumped off him and tried to run but he held her down until he too felt the origin of her excitement.

Whap, whap, whap! Ivan had taken all that he

could stomach and removed his belt and gave the
naughty two the beaten they deserved. Angelica had
jumped forward to the head of the bed, turning around
to see what was happening and Ivan continued to pelt
Dr. Painkin with the hard leather belt. Painkin fought
to get up reaching out for the belt but couldn't grab it.
He continued to receive the lashes until he had finally
rolled over and off the bed. Ivan was right behind him
continuing to punish him for his wrongful act.

"You two have been naughty. Did you know that
God doesn't look favorably on an act like this? This is
my wife for crying out loud!" He said with amusement.

Painkin's hardened member which stood so high
and strong had shriveled to about the size of a triple A
battery. If it could shrink any further, it would have.
Finally, Painkin had taken enough abuse and rushed
forward to attack Ivan. Ivan swiped Painkin with the
scalpel Tammy was so gracious to leave him. Even in
death, she was still helping him. He took a moment to
remember her. She would have made a good partner
and lover.

Painkin squealed from the biting pain of the
sharpest knife in the world. That thing could cut
straight to the bone without any effort on the user's
part. He looked down to see what kind of damage was
done. His flesh opened revealing tissue and muscle.
Blood ran like tears from the opening.

Angelica watched in fear. Wanting to help but she
knew that her efforts would be futile. Painkin grabbed
a towel and applied pressure to his abdomen trying to
slow down the bleeding.

Ivan laughed chanting "Olay." Painkin was like a
charging bull that realized that his charging was effort-
less and defeat was eminent. He waited to see if he
wanted to dance anymore.

"Come on, you mean to tell me that you brought my angel all the way out here to die without even the slightest fight for her.   Certainly she deserves more than that. Look how many people I have killed for her. In fact, the two officers that arrested me were just as shocked as you are right now. I had surrendered so easily they didn't even bother checking me. I accepted the bracelets humbly, got into the special chariot they came to pick me up in and finally, I listened to their fairy tales about how they saved the day. They never asked themselves who would save their day. Anyway, enough about me. Dr. Painkin so tell me, how did the two of you decide to hook up?"

Dr. Painkin didn't answer. He continued applying pressure to the opening.

"What you got there?   I'm sure it's nothing you can't fix. I mean, look at my angel. Doesn't she look great? Even for you that's remarkable. Not even the old scars are there. Plastic surgery?"

The pain intensified as the wound became more exposed to the air. It tingled.

Ivan turned his attention back to Angelica.

"I guess the doctor here has been doing you well huh. Come here and let me see if you taste as good as you used to."

He grabbed her by the arm and Painkin hurled the crystal vase across the bed, striking Ivan's temple. It broke on impact and he laughed.

"Shit man. You just cut me. What? You don't want me to have a little taste of my own stuff."

"She doesn't want you. Why don't you just leave her alone?" Painkin told Ivan through gasps.

"No can do man. She will have to die before I leave here. I married her." Ivan grabbed Angelica's leg as she tried to escape again. He pressed her bottom against his jean covered organ.

"Don't worry my angel, I won't leave you hanging like the doctor did. I know what you want."

He banged against her, cutting her flesh with his zipper.

"Care to watch?" he asked Painkin who was trying to decide how to proceed. Ivan started to open his zipper so that he could enter her when Painkin jumped across the bed running into the nose of a 38.

"Getting a little rambunctious aren't you doctor? I was just wondering how fast you'd heal from a bullet wound!"

Angelica kicked him and he fell back letting off one shot as he hit the floor. The bullet struck Painkin in the neck and he collapsed on the bed.

Nooooo!" She screamed as the blood shot out in spurts. He was losing blood fast and she knew that this one was going to do it. Ivan quickly jumped up and hurried over to Angelica, pushed her out the way and fired two more shots into him. Finally his struggling was at peace and his fight was over. Ivan pushed him to the floor and grabbed his wife...

"Now where were we?" She was screaming and pleading uncontrollably. He rendered a quick slap to calm her down. He pushed her down on the bed and again prepared to take what he felt belonged to him.

❦

Meanwhile Painkin slipping closer and closer to darkness, noticed someone approaching him and he thought..." their pretty quick." At first he was afraid because he didn't know what to expect but when he saw him, he knew that this would be an easy ride. Of course, he thought it would be a beautiful woman to get him like the ones he saw in the movies.

"Steve, Angelica is in trouble and you can't help her

like this. You are about to die and I need you to save her."

"Who are you?"

"Something you will never comprehend, but I love her just as much as you do and I can give her back to you if you agree to give me your body."

The statement took him by surprise and he wondered why he didn't just take it.

"Are you the one who saved her in the operating room?"

"Yes. And I will save her now if you don't waste time. I have been around for a very long time, watching over her and now we can bring her nightmare to an end if you ask with your lips. You know if you had only called the police from the start, you would not have caused the needless deaths of your medical staff."

"You told me to protect her. I was only trying to protect her."

"You humans and your inflated egos are still far from divinity. How could you believe that doing something wrong would make Angelica's situation right?"

Painkin gave a chuckle. "This is a fine time to tell me when I'm lying here bleeding to death. Her monster husband is about to rape her, then kill her. Why couldn't you just give me super hero powers?"

"You are so perfect for Angelica. You have a great sense of humor, but now is hardly the time for that."

"Well, I thought I should get that in before I start up that lit passage over there."

The shadow turned around to see what Painkin was talking about.

"You're staring at a light bulb. There is no bright light. So, stop with this self pity and let's save her. I will show you the divine power of God. Will me in Steve."

"What do I have to say? Will I still be me? Will I

die afterwards? I don't want to trick her and put her into the hands of someone else."

"We will both have her. We don't have much time! Say it."

Painkin swallowed his fear and trusted his inner voice and uttered in the last voice he had...

"Use me."

Then with a jerk, his life left him. Ivan thought he heard something and stopped to see what was going on. Painkin remained on the floor in a puddle of blood, dying for the sins he committed. Then Painkin stood up. Ivan stood there in shock wondering how a man dead only a moment ago, full of bullet holes get up as though nothing had happened to him.

"Angelica, I want you to go downstairs. I will take care of Ivan once and for all. He has committed a great sin against too many people and will have to pay for all of them now. He will never harm you again."

Without questioning, Angelica hurried out the room. Ivan didn't attempt to stop her as something beyond his understanding was happening and he didn't quite know how to handle it. He fired the last two shots to no avail. Painkin stood there and his body illuminated. The light from his body lit up the entire room and the stairway that Angelica fought to descend. She wondered what Painkin was going to do to Ivan but she wouldn't look back remembering the story of Lot and his wife from the Bible.

"Ivan, I have come to punish you for the crimes against Angelica and all the others you have tormented and murdered."

Ivan shuddered for the first time in his life besides when his father called him. He needed answers.

"Who are you?"

"I am the Dark Angel. I am the bringer of death to

those who can not be punished by the law. I am going to take your life and give it to the one you just took."

"Why are you after me? I'm not the only one whose committed murder. There are murderers all over the world."

"Yes and they too will suffer. But today is your turn."

He placed his hands on Ivan's head and into him came all the plagues he's given to others. His body fell to the floor and started jerking uncontrollably. The shadow watched him yell and scream as he felt the kicks, punches and the gasping for oxygen while his hands squeezed his own throat. His eye felt a sudden burn and blood poured from it, then a sharp pain to the back of his head. He felt the stings of leather lashing out at him, but there was no belt to be seen. Then he felt the worst of it. He lifted his shirt to see a long gash ripping through his skin, exposing his muscles. He yelled in agony, pleading for mercy, begging for help, praying for death.

"God, I'm sorry. Please forgive me. Angelica, forgive me," he screamed. "Please forgive me."

Angelica had never heard such pleading and wondered what was going on. Steve was dead and she knew it. How this could be happening, she wondered. As much as she wanted to know, she was afraid to see. Apparently it was something that wasn't meant for her eyes or something she could not understand.

Ivan continued to feel the pain. With each new pain, he saw the faces of Barbara Givens, Geneva of Seven Eleven, Carol from the hospital, Richard, Nurse Green, Tammy, the two officers, and Dr. Painkin. Then he wondered, why he saw his face if he wasn't dead. It was as though bullets were being fired at him. He felt the punches followed by the burning and knew that it had to be bullets.

Painkin's arms were outstretched and the injuries that Ivan had inflicted him with started healing as they left his body and entered Ivan's. Ivan body continued to feel the pain. He asked for forgiveness, but it was too late. The crimes were committed and there was no way he could give back the lives he had taken. When he had finally felt the last of his punishment, his body ceased to live. There was nothing left of him which was recognizable. The shadow had allowed him to live through everything he had inflicted so that even in death he would not win.

The Shadow stepped out of Painkin's body. He was healed. Looking at the body laying on the floor, there was blood everywhere. Ivan was practically unrecognizable. His fingerprints alone would identify him. But where he was going, this was only the beginning of his punishment. The life that was ode here was given back. The shadow had given to Painkin the life he didn't cherish. Now it was up to him to love Angelica and give her the life she deserved. When all was completed, the shadow spoke to Painkin...

"I am leaving now, and you will never see me again. My job here is done."

"I have a question for you before you leave. How is it that you were able to help Angelica in the operating room?"

"You asked me too. You just didn't realize that you would be answered."

"Thank you."

"What about Ivan's body. How will I explain it?"

"Ivan's body will not be here, I will take what's left of him with me. He is far from paying his debt. Take care of Angelica. She is a beautiful woman. It's too bad I can't have her."

"What are you exactly?"

"This is something you can never know. I am, and will always be lurking in the shadows waiting to right the wrong."

Painkin saw the shadow as he walked away from him. Right then, he knew that he was being given another chance just as Angelica was. Someone had also given her their life, but no one will ever know just where it came from. When the Shadow had disappeared, he hurried downstairs to where Angelica was...

"Honey, are you all right?" Angelica asked as she ran into his open arms. She traced his chest where the wounds were, confirming that they were gone.

"I'm fine. What just happened?"

"Let's just say its over and we can go on with our lives. I love you."

"I love you too."

"So, how about that vacation I promised you?"

She smiled and turned to go upstairs to grab some clothes.

"No need for that. Let's just get out of here."

The two of them simultaneously looked back at the room at the top of the stairs both knowing that what had happened should never be talked about but definitely remembered. The shadow watched as the two of them left the house, knowing that he would never see her again but she would be happy. They both needed each other each for their own reasons.

When they had gotten into the car. Angelica cupped his face in her hands, staring deep into his eyes and said... "Yes!"

Painkin grabbed her up into his arms and kissed her, then asked... "Big?"

"Small."

"Two?"

"Three."

"New house?"

"Definitely."

Now In Stores

Best Seller

What lurks between these pages can kill you!

Kurt Daley, an aspiring writer, gets more than she bargains for when her favorite bestselling author, Dean, hands her a possession he is dying to pass on.

Dean's new protégé, Kurt, will fulfill her destiny and write the greatest best-seller ever—a dreadful tale that reaches out and touches everyone close to her. It isn't long before the accomplished writer finds herself living out a perilous tale of her own.

Now Kurt Daley will have to find the secrets hidden behind being a best-seller before the clock runs out.

What if you knew that everyone page you wrote brought you closer to your end?

Now In Stores
Not With My Son

Keesha Smalls has been out of passion's game for a long time until she takes a second look at her best friend's son. The dashingly gorgeous Chris Walker brings more than flaming romance to Keesha's bedroom. Their secret romance is perfect until Christine, Chris' mother finds out.

A mother's rage can be terrifying but someone's past can be deadly. Keesha learns that sometimes it's better to have never known love than to love the wrong man.

Preview the sequel to
Not With My Son
Vengeance Is Mine

"04673, you got a visitor."

Michelle dismounted her cot and moved towards the cell bars and faced the correction officer.

"Who is it?" she questioned with a slightly raspy tone. She stared at the officer, waiting for a response. His lips twisted into half cocked smile exposing an exaggerated overbite.

"Chris Walker."

The mention of his name brought pause. And why shouldn't it? She's been in this cage for Ten years and it's been just that long since she's seen her daughter, their daughter. Chris vowed to her moments after her delivery that she would never see Ashley again. She held her daughter only moments before she was taken away from her for what would be, forever.

"Yes or no 04673?" he insisted, snapping her out of her trance.

"Yes. I'll see him."

"Let's go," he instructed manually opening her cell door. He escorted her to the awaiting female officer. She was taken to the shower to clean up. After a thorough search, Michelle quickly dressed and followed her escort to the visitor's room. This would be Michelle's first time having a visitor and she didn't know what to expect. When the doors were opened for her, the desk officer went over the rules with her, and then directed her to her seat. This was better than she expected as she thought that she would have a Plexiglas between them and a telephone. She was seated at a table with four seats to it. Surrounding her was approximately a hundred other female inmates with their guests. Some were at vending machines buying pre-packaged food while others were using the microwave. Officers were stationed throughout the cafeteria with direct eyeshot of everything.

After sitting there for more than twenty minutes, Chris walked in with a group of other people. They handed a form to the officer at the door and were then instructed to their party. Michelle could feel her heart racing as he closed the distance between them. He was as handsome as ever. Time had matured him well. She could also see that he had put on a little weight, in a good way. His muscles were bigger as well as his chest. He wore a Grey, short-sleeve, nylon shirt that clung to every ripple of his tight stomach. The black Italian cut pants fell seductively over his perfectly firm ass.

He stopped as he reached the table, taking in a full view of Michelle. Although Ten years had passed; ten hard years, she still maintained her beauty. Of course with the exception of the scar that lingered just above her eyebrow. He could see that she had been working out on a regular and her body was a bit less feminine but attractive none-the-less. She wore her hair in long braids that fell down her back and rested probably six or seven inches above her butt.

"Are you going to sit down? Or are you going to stand there and observe me all day?" A grin spilled across her face as she noted his embarrassment.

"Sorry. I'm going to sit down."

"You look well." She stated as he got comfortable.

He cleared his throat.

"So do you."

Chris looked around observing all the women in the facility. He then focused his attention on the officers holding the guns at the doors.

"Not really a friendly place is it?"

"It's a prison Chris. Did you think I was on vacation here?" she remarked no longer yielding her sarcasm and annoyance. "Why are you here? And where is my daughter?"

"Ashley is fine. She's a beautiful young girl."

"I'm sure. But that doesn't answer my first question." Her eyes never left his.

Chris shifted in his seat, leaned forward and rested his

clasped hands on the table.

"Ashley has been asking about her mother lately. She wants to meet you."

His words were labored since the thought went against his wishes. But his love for Ashley was enough to make him go against his promise. He would give her anything she asked for to make her happy. Things were so simple when she was an infant growing into a toddler, but now that she is among older children and they talk about their parents, Ashley has become obsessed with knowing her mother.

Michelle narrowed her eyes at Chris. He was still that selfish bastard he was Ten years ago when he disregarded her feelings for him.

"Did you think that you could take my daughter and turn her against me? No State paper can break the bond a mother has with her child. She was with me in the beginning and so shall she be in the end. That bond can not be broken Chris. Maybe from your perspective it could be broken. I mean you did abandon yours."

Chris first instinct was to punch her lights out, but being surrounded by shotguns wouldn't make that choice prudent. He shifted back in his seat, glaring at her. Michelle could see the tension building between them. Chris once relaxed muscles became taut making the vesicles more pronounce including the ones in his neck.

"You know that look isn't appealing," she added to his fury.

"By the way, did you ever make partner? You know at Goldman, Thurman & Sacs? You look like you're pretty well off."

Chris didn't respond. He couldn't believe how cold and vicious Michelle had become. Did she feel any remorse for what she'd done? Or over the life she'd taken? How many years would it take for her to realize that what she did was wrong? She's got some nerve asking about his daughter, his Ashley when she was so willing to let her be raised by the State. When the Social Worker called him and told him that his daughter would be turned over to the State, Chris immediately hurried to the hospital, awaiting the arrival of his daughter. Shortly after she was born, Chris began the paperwork to get full custody of his daughter and remove any possibility of Michelle ever seeing his daughter.

"Michelle to Chris. Are you there? It's not even fun talking to you. You're like a zombie. Well, since you didn't bring my daughter, I think you should be leaving now."

Chris stood from his seat and casually returned the seat beneath the table.

"I can't say that seeing you again was a pleasure."

"Don't worry. You'll see a lot of me soon. My appeal is just around the corner."

"I look forward to the battle. You will never have my daughter. And you will pay for your transgressions."

"I've spent Ten years here. I have paid for my transgressions."

"No. I mean your transgression against me and my mother."

"You have no proof that I killed your mother."

"You did it. I know you did it."

"Well, the court system found me innocent on that charge."

"But I find you guilty."

"Thanks for taking care of my daughter for me. I'll see you two soon." She called out to him.

He turned and walked away. He returned to the officer at the door and retrieved his pass. After a few moments, he disappeared through the steel door where they checked for a stamp on his hand.

When Chris returned to the waiting area, his girlfriend, Simone and daughter, Ashley stood to greet him. Her hair was curly like her fathers and pulled into two ponytails that bounced at the sides of her head. Ashley was excited because she knew that Chris would be bringing her in to meet her mother. He told her to wait with Simone until he saw her first and that he would return to get her as soon as he talked with her.

Chris took a seat and caught hold of Ashley's hand. He

kissed both of them and told her how much he loved her and would do anything in this world for her. All of his emotions surged forward and his tears exposed the hurt he felt. He continued to hold her hands, never letting his eyes meet hers.

"What happened Dad? Why are you crying?"

"Honey. Your mom." He stammered.

Simone could see that something went wrong. Chris never told her the whole story about Michelle and how Ashley came about. He only told her that her mother was locked up and that she was sentenced to ten to twenty years. Simone worked as a Social Worker and was the one who contacted Chris about his daughter. She helped him gain legal custody of Ashley. Chris was surprised at how easy the process had been for him to get Ashley. Simone was somehow able to get Michelle to sign the papers giving Chris sole custody of their daughter. Not long after, Chris and Simone began seeing each other. She reminded Chris so much of Keesha, sweet, gentle, caring and so desperately in need of love. Her companionship was so timely as Chris had no idea how he was going to raise Ashley by himself. Simone took to Ashley as if she was her own daughter. Strangely though, Simone never mentioned marriage after being together for seven years. They still maintained their separate places. Simone would spend some weekends Chris and Ashley and other times, Ashley would stay with Simone for weekends. This was their bonding time to do their girl thing.

She rested her hands gently on Ashley's shoulders.

"Come on sweet heart, let's wait for your dad in the car. We'll come out another day to see your mom. She wasn't feeling well today."

Ashley hesitated for a moment then followed Simone outside to the car.

While Simone escorted Ashley out, Chris could hear their conversation.

"Simone how do you know that my mom is sick?" Simone's responded by saying that Chris told her that she wasn't feeling well before they left, but he didn't know how sick she was. "Don't worry, your dad said hello to your mom for you and she knows that you love her."

Chris pulled himself together before getting into the car.

"How are my two angels doing?" he said forcing a big smile.

"Will mom be okay dad?"

"Sure Honey. She's just got a really bad cold and she told me to give you a big hug for her and tell you that she will see you soon."

Chris pulled Ashley into his arms and squeezed her tight.

"Mom's coming home soon? She's going to live with us?"

Instinctively, Chris eyes met Simone's then he looked back at his awaiting daughter.

"Honey, your mom and I will have separate homes. She won't live with us, but you can see her from time to time."

He started the car and they were on their way home. The ride was quiet. Chris asked Simone if it would be okay if he took her home and that he needed time to talk with his daughter. She didn't feel his request to be prudent, but she reluctantly nodded her head and focused her attention out the window until Chris entered her driveway.

"Ashley, sweetheart, come give me a kiss."

Ashley sat up in her seat and puckered her lips and gave Simone a big kiss.

"I'll see you tomorrow or over the weekend okay?"

"Dad why isn't Simone coming to the house? I don't want her to go home."

"I know honey, but your dad want to spend time with you and talk to you about some really important stuff that can't wait. Simone will come over tomorrow and she will be around for a very long time. How is that?" He said while winking at Simone in an effort to make light of a very tense situation.

"Okay dad. See you tomorrow Simone. Love you." She called out to her as she closed the door and stepped out of the way of the car.

"You want to sit up front with your dad?"

"Sure."

Chris waited for Ashley to come to the front seat. When she had buckled herself in, Chris waved to Simone then started toward home.

He pulled into the driveway of his mother's home. After all that had happened, it became his sanctuary. Although Christine was gone, he could still feel her presence upon entering what was once her home, his home. He did, of course, modernize some things Christine neglected to repair or update. It made a suitable home for him and Ashley. So many memories remained that he wanted to share about his mother, her grandmother.

Upon entering, Ashley raced upstairs to her bedroom. Chris had decorated it with pink wallpaper with tiny pastel hearts on it. The square room was filled with teddy bears, Barbie dolls, a canopy bed with Barbie accessories. She also had Barbie furniture including a vanity, where she often sat and imagined growing up to look like her mother. Chris didn't talk much about her mother, and neither did he want to. He only told her that her mother had gone away, and would be away for a very long time.

She sat at her vanity looking at herself in the mirror, clutching a teddy her dad had given her on her third birthday. The fur was so soft and plush. Today was disappointing. She had told her classmates that she was going to see her mother this weekend and that she was going to live with her and her father. Why didn't mommy want to see me? She wondered. Why would dad not let me see her?

Ashley felt empty inside. Although Chris went over and beyond to make her happy, and Simone was like a mother to her, the desire to be with her real mother still existed. She thought of Simone as a really cool person. She was fun to be with, but she was not her mother. She found that out on her seventh birthday during an argument she had with her father. A lot changed between them since that agreement. Simone didn't keep Ashley overnight as often as she had in the past, but she did come over on a regular and they still enjoyed the mall during the day. Chris was over protective of Ashley and he seemed to be afraid of losing her.

Chris climbed the stairs quietly. He knew that Ashley was upset and that now was the time to explain to her where her mother is and why. He looked into her room. He remembered the day he brought her home from the hospital. As much as he hated Michelle, he could not live with himself if her let his daughter be placed in a foster home for ten years until her mother was released from jail and was able to care for her. She was adorable the moment he laid eyes on her. She had a head full of dark curly hair that seemed overwhelming for her tiny face, nothing that a brush couldn't tame.

He silently walked over to her and knelt by her side. When she lifted her head, her eyes were soaked with tears. The sight melted his heart. What am I going to tell her to help her understand? I can't tell her that her mother is a crazed killer or that the grandmother she never had is dead because her mother ended her life. Or that I want to kill her for ruining my life.

"Hey, what are all the tears about?"

"The kids at school won't believe me if I tell them that I have a mother."

"Of course you have a mother. How do you think you got here? Huh? Come here."

Chris cuddled her for a moment and then walked her over to her bed. He sat her down beside him then turned her chin to face him. It was like looking into a mirror. She is a total replica of him. She had his eyes, his nose, his complexion, his hair, his lips, everything.

"Honey, there are some things that I need to tell you. I don't want to because it is something that I wanted to protect you from, but I'm afraid that if I don't tell you, I may lose you."

"You can never lose me daddy."